Adventures Beyond the Fence

The Cove

By: KENT ARCENEAUX

Dedication

This book is dedicated to Robert F. Einstein Sr., My father-in law who passed away earlier this year. Robert and I shared in the joy and blessing of raising daughters and our undying need to protect them.

Robert was a loving father, husband, grandfather and the epitome of a true Christian. He is missed dearly by everyone he knew and his spirit still lives within his kids and family to carry on his legacy.

Acknowledgments

I would like to acknowledge those that, without their help, this book would not have been possible. Thank you to my mentor, Don Massenzio, who forced me to come out of my shell and believe in myself as a writer.

Thank you to my new friend and editor Catherine Violando. Her patience and attention to detail were crucial to the completion of this book.

A special thanks to artist and illustrator, Bart Bergeron for the included pictures to help bring this book to life.

Thank you to my friends, family and especially my mom, Brenda Fanguy for tireless reading and helping me along the way.

Finally, thank you to my wife, Shannon for her undying patience and support to allow me to see this project through. You and our girls are my true inspiration to continue to provide, protect and love with all that I have.

Praise for Frank Immersed

My first attempt at writing was a co-write with Author Don Massenzio, where he allowed me to join him in the Frank Rozzani series. It was an honor and pleasure writing with him. These are a few of the reviews we received.

"Don Massenzio and Kent Arceneaux team up on this latest Detective Rozzani novel and deliver a perfect strike. A fast, fun read that'll make you circle back to the others in the series if you haven't already read them or wanting more if you have."

"Very well written thriller with an excellent plot and great realistic characters. There is plenty of action and the storyline provides for a quick enjoyable read. A book that has a great conclusion. I would definitely recommend this book to family and friends."

"Absolutely loved this book! What a great Mystery story! It was definitely a book I could not put down. It kept me engaged from cover to cover! I definitely recommend this book to everyone!"

"The laughter and imagination of a child should never be suppressed or discarded, it is what makes them into the artist they will become."

Kent Arceneaux

Prologue

The MD-80 bounced vigorously through the air, hitting pockets of turbulence as the pilot attempted to land at the Louis Armstrong New Orleans International Airport in Louisiana. The weather forecast indicated scattered showers and possible thunderstorms upon arrival when Dirk checked it for the fifth time before takeoff. At fifty years old, flying wasn't his favorite thing to do, and with every rise and fall of the aircraft, he gasped for air. The multiple drinks he had consumed at the Orlando Sanford International Airport did not have the effect he had been hoping for. He was wide awake and gripping the armrests like they were the only thing keeping him from dropping out of the sky like a rock. Dirk instantly regretted his decision to fly home for the meeting. He hadn't been home since his father's funeral in 1992, and he had driven that time.

"Twenty-four years, my how time flies!" he whispered under his breath as he glanced out of the small window, which was partially obscured by a plastic shade. Choosing a window seat was another decision he regretted. As he lowered the shade, he caught a glimpse of Lake Pontchartrain, one thousand feet below and a flurry of bad scenarios entered his mind.

The plane banked hard to the left as it circled over the lake and took its final position for a northern approach. Dirk closed his eyes and held his breath for what felt like an eternity, until he felt the jarring impact of the wheels touch down onto the runway. The reverse thrust of the engines combined with the brakes propelled him forward a little, and the force of the seatbelt was uncomfortable across his waist. He readjusted in his seat, took a long much needed breath, and opened his eyes. Another successful flight under his belt, he thought. The older he became, the more uneasy he felt when flying. Dirk felt that the more he flew, the closer he was to his luck running out. He had nightmares about it.

The pilot taxied the plane to a stop at the assigned gate and the rat race of getting off the plane and retrieving luggage began. Dirk waited patiently in seat 36D and knew it would be a while before he moved. He purposely requested the last seat on the plane after researching the safest place to sit while flying and was happy to wait. He raised the shade on the window, placed his Costa sunglasses over his eyes and noticed the workers hustling around with the baggage. As he watched two men place a ladder under the left wing, his mind drifted off to a much simpler time.

– – – – – – – –

"Go ahead and step through." Jerry said. "I'm not lying. You'll see!"

Dirk did what he was told not because of peer pressure from Jerry, but because he was curious. The fence was rusted barbed wire threaded along old weathered posts that were spaced eight feet apart. It stretched from old man Murphy's property, all the way to the Intracoastal Waterway. It covered three hundred acres of woods and cow pastures, to be exact- an endless playground for two young boys. The property beyond the fence was owned by the Thompsons and they kept a pretty good eye on it.

Jerry placed his thumbs under the top wire to lift it and put his muddy toes on the lower one to hold it down. It had rained quite a bit lately, and the well-traveled path that was once grass had now turned into a pile of slop. Dirk bent down low and slid through the opening, careful not to catch his sweatshirt on the barbs. When his entire body was on the other side, everything changed.

The view from the other side of the fence before he crossed over, looked nothing like this. From there, he could see the three-stall barn surrounded by black iron fencing used to herd the cows, tall ryegrass with spots of mud puddles throughout, and two cattle guards protecting the dirt roads from the animals on either side of the pasture. They had spent countless days slipping under the door of the barn and tunneling through the large hay bales for a game of hide-and-seek. He and Jerry played chase on the fence and if your feet touched the ground, you were out of the game and the next person, it. They did this without permission, and the possibility of a slight trespassing charge added to the excitement. The owner of the property would frequently drive through on his three-wheeler to check on things and chase them to the other side of the fence with a threat to call their parents. He never did.

The scenery was different now. It still had all the same items-the barn, the fence the grass and the dirt roads, but it all felt different somehow. It was brighter, warmer, and the colors seemed to be more vibrant. Jerry wasn't lying and was quick to follow through the fence just to see the sheer excitement on his best friend's face.

"What just happened?" Dirk asked.

"I told you so" Jerry said, smiling as he watched Dirk's expression quickly change from doubt to belief.

"What is this place?" Dirk asked as he gazed around.

"It's whatever you want it to be," Jerry said as he shrugged his shoulders and continued. "Come on. I'll show you."

Jerry shouldered the backpack and led the way down the well, worn path through the long winter ryegrass. Dirk turned back to look at the fence and, surprisingly, it continued as far as he could see and vanished into a haze of fog. He didn't understand. From the other side, the fence only went as far as old Murphy's farm, which was only a few hundred yards. This fence seemed to stretch on forever. It didn't make sense to him because he knew the area quite well, or so he thought.

On the other side of the fence, the weather was overcast and cool, but on this side the sun was shining so brightly that it felt like a hot summer day. It reminded him of the kind of day they would go sneak and swim in the bayou back behind the Murphy's place. They called it sneak swimming because without their parent's permission, they would leave a change of clothes hanging in the trees and change before returning home. The walk home was just long enough for the sun to dry their hair and their system worked every time. Beads of sweat were already forming on Dirk's forehead and it didn't take long before he realized he had overdressed for this place. Dirk shucked off his hoody to cool off a bit and tied the long sleeves around his waist as he followed close behind Jerry.

"Where are we going?" Dirk's curiosity pleaded.

"Just follow me and be quiet, you don't want to wake the bull."

"The bull?" Dirk asked.

Suddenly the pounding of hooves shook the ground behind them and Jerry smiled and started running. The sound of a heavy bellow was getting closer and Dirk could see something coming towards them. He knew that sound and had heard it many times before when he watched his uncle branding cattle.

"Run Dirk!" Jerry screamed as he ran down the path, took a quick right through the tall blood weed and headed for the trees that lined the bayou. Dirk was right on his heels as they made their way to the trees and stopped once they reached the muddy bank of the Intracoastal. Jerry turned back to look at the field and as fast as it appeared, it was gone. It always disappeared when he got to the trees. Dirk stood bent over with his hands on his knees trying to catch his breath and managed to speak.

"What the heck was that?" He asked gasping for air.

"I told you. Whatever you want it to be." Jerry said. "I wanted to show you how it worked so I thought of a bull and actually said the word out loud."

"What? That's crazy!" Dirk said as he stood up straight and tried to understand.

"I know it's crazy, but it's real." Jerry went on as he picked up a rock and skimmed it across the muddy water. "I don't understand it either. Just be glad you weren't here when I said tiger, I almost didn't make it to the trees." Jerry looked up at the branches as the sunlight glimmered through the leaves. "This seems to be some sort of safe place. Nothing happens in the trees, only the pasture."

"So, you're telling me that whatever you think of and say, appears here?" Dirk asked with still a little tone of disbelief.

"Yes, it does." Jerry said.

"So why didn't you say mouse, or rabbit?"

"It wouldn't have been as fun." Jerry laughed with an evil chuckle and threw another rock. Dirk watched as the rock skipped across the water and noticed that it kept skipping.

"How did you do that? You barely threw it."

"I'm not sure, but it does it every time. There are so many amazing things here Dirk. Sometimes I don't want to go home." Jerry said and looked for some sort of a response from his best friend.

Dirk ignored his last statement and continued to question.

"How did you find this place?" He asked with a wrinkled forehead.

"By accident. Did you notice the section of fence we came through had different colored posts?"

"No!" Dirk answered.

"Well, they are different. All the other posts are black and white and look old. Those two, look brand new. I didn't notice it at first either. You know we have crossed that fence hundreds of times and nothing changed. I guess we just never crossed right there. Last week I was chasing a lizard down the fence and decided to cross in between those two. That's when I found it."

"How many times have you been here?" Dirk asked.

Jerry lowered his head like he was ashamed to answer.

13

"Every day since I found it. I can't help it. I feel different when I'm in here. I feel, important."

"Who else knows about this?" Dirk, asked concerned for their safety, but more so to be alone with his friend and a secret.

"As far as I know, just us. All I've seen back here is animals that I've imagined up. And some other things." Jerry answered and then there was a pause.

"What other things?" Dirk was more curious.

"It doesn't matter." Jerry seemed to be agitated by the question and started to walk along the bank of the bayou.

"What other things?" Dirk persisted as he followed.

Jerry stopped suddenly and turned to face his friend.

"Do you promise not to say anything to anyone?" Jerry asked with wild eyes.

"Yes, I promise!" Dirk pleaded.

"Hope to die, stick a needle in your eye and pinky swear?"

Jerry held his hand up with his pinky extended.

"Yes, I promise and pinky swear!" Dirk said as they made their ritual pinky shake.

Jerry looked around like he was worried someone would overhear and lowered his voice.

"Do you remember the little girl that was visiting at the Murphy's two summers ago and disappeared?

"The one they said possibly drowned back here in the bayou and they never found?" Dirk whispered back.

"Yes!"

"Yea, what about her?" Dirk pressed.

"Follow me." Jerry said.

CHAPTER 1

Jerry Davis was 12 years old and like most boys who grew up in the bayous of South Louisiana, was more comfortable outside in the woods and water than being stuck inside his home. Shoes were also something that he had to wear to school, but rarely found his feet when he wasn't there, playing sports or in church. He spent most of his time running through the woods or playing football into the late evening. Jerry learned very early on from his older siblings that when darkness fell, he should be within calling distance of his mother's voice from the front porch. Although darkness didn't always mean it was time to come home, it did mean you should be close to finishing up. The streetlights often illuminated the neighborhood football game that just couldn't finish with a tie. Almost on cue, the mothers would make the dinner calls and within minutes the shoes were gathered, the scores were tallied, and the kids would call for a rematch before beginning their trek home.

Jerry was the youngest of eight kids and the most spoiled if you asked his siblings. Maybe because after raising that many kids his parents were just too worn down to say no anymore. He had plenty of friends and cousins in the neighborhood, but it wasn't uncommon to find him spending most of his time with his best friend Dirk. They had known each other practically from birth. Their mothers had them one day apart and two rooms away from each other at the local hospital.

Dirk Matherne was slightly taller than Jerry and carried a little more weight. The two of them were inseparable and often spent consecutive days and nights at each other's homes. Jerry's mom had often joked that Dirk was her adopted son and threatened to claim him on her taxes.

They went to the same schools, played on the same sports teams and shared in the mischief of being young. So, in the winter of 1978 when Jerry told Dirk he had something secret to show him, there was no hesitation in the decision to take a look. They packed some snacks in a backpack and Jerry grabbed a few items from his room. They left the house and told Mrs. Davis they would be home before supper.

The Davis home was built in the late 1930's and was once the home of a cotton farmer in the area. It had wood siding with a tin roof and window units supplied the air conditioning. It was three bedrooms and one bathroom which wasn't uncommon in these times. The bedrooms were separated into the girl's room, the boy's room, which had two bunk beds and a trundle and finally a modest sized master bedroom for the parents. The house was originally situated on twenty acres of land which had been split into parcels and sold separately by the family before them. Chicken coops lined the back-yard fence and clothes was always hanging out to dry on the line constructed by Mr. Davis. They had a washer and dryer, but with ten people in the house, it was impossible to dry everything inside.

Jerry and Dirk made their way through the back yard and kicked dirt at a rooster that had found his way out of the coop. He flared his wings for a second and started to attack their shoes, but changed his mind and scampered away when Jerry's dog joined into the fight. Jerry told Red, his retriever, to stay in the yard as they exited through the back gate.

The weather was turning cooler and the leaves that could, had started to change color. Some of them had already fallen and began to collect in piles. The two of them walked side by side, kicked the piles of leaves in unison and whistled a horrible rendition of The Andy Griffith Show. As they continued to walk towards the old barn, they talked about sports and of course who they thought were the prettiest girls at school. Dirk swore it was Rebecca Smith, but Jerry disagreed and said hands down the prettiest girl on earth was Shannon Einstein. They argued about it for a while until Jerry changed the subject and asked the weirdest question Dirk had ever heard from his best friend.

"Do you believe in magical places?"

"What do you mean like, Wizard of Oz like places?" Dirk asked baffled by the question.

"Like places you never thought existed, but actually do?"

"I don't know? Never really thought about it, to be honest. Why?"

They stopped at the long, barbed wire fence that separated their property from the Thompson's.

"I told you I had a secret to show you. It's right here on the other side of this fence." "What is it? I don't see anything that I usually don't see. There's the barn, the cattle fencing and the troughs that feed the cows. What are you talking about?" Dirk asked with frustration.

"It's on the other side of the fence. You just can't see it from this side." Jerry explained. "There is a magical place on the other side."

"Yea, ok? Whatever!"

@@@@@

Bourg, Louisiana was a small town situated about an hour Southwest of New Orleans with a population of nearly 5,000 people. Most of the city was located in Terrebonne Parish with a few parcels in the neighboring parish of Lafourche. The man-made Intracoastal Canal bordered the north-west side of Bourg and created a shipping pathway from New Orleans through Houma to the West of Louisiana. The canal was riddled with work barges and tug boats pushing supplies to support the oilfield. These boats and barges also provided a dangerous lure for kids and quite often when they were tied up for repair along the canal, they became high diving platforms for them.

In the summer of 1976 tragedy struck the small town of Bourg, Louisiana when a young girl from out of town went missing on the Thompson's land. Penny Myers was visiting her Uncle Murphy for the summer while her parents had business in Paris. She was last seen crossing through the fence behind her Uncle's farm and when she didn't return, she was believed to have drowned. The local police, neighbors and the National Guard searched the bayou and swamp for weeks and never found her. Bulletins and pictures of Penny were circulated all throughout South Louisiana and not one shred of evidence turned up. The police received the usual possible sightings here and there, but nothing concrete ever surfaced.

They also investigated the Murphy's and turned the farm upside down looking for her, but found nothing there as well. It had been two years since she disappeared and no one had seen or heard anything from her. She went into the endless file of missing teens and the chance of finding her now was dismal at best. It didn't take long before the rumors started that old man Murphy's son Michael had something to do with the disappearance. He was 17 years old and mentally delayed. Deprived from oxygen when his umbilical cord was tangled during birth, he would never be like the other kids and the rest of his life would be a challenge for him and his family. He had the mind of a much younger child and was often seen playing a little too rough with the younger kids, not understanding his strength. When Michael was interviewed about the girl, he lost control and started beating himself. Eventually the Murphy's had to hire an attorney to ward off the media and to protect themselves from their own family. When the Myers returned from Paris after hearing the news of their missing daughter, the first thing they did after they mourned was point the finger at Michael. Knowing the financial situation of Jack Murphy, they sued the uncle for damages and won.

The rumors of Michael being involved in the disappearance returned and the pressure from the Myer's and the public, forced the authorities to dig deeper. They questioned Michael again with a psychologist present this time and his violent reactions to the questions about Penny resulted in permanent confinement to a mental facility.

When the dust settled, Mr. Murphy became somewhat of a recluse and was constantly running people off his land, especially kids using his land as a pathway to fishing spots and swimming holes. The Murphy's place which was once a bustling, productive farm, now looked more like a place of dismal emptiness. The landscaping that was once pristine and inviting was overgrown and smothered the main house to be nearly invisible. At the end of a dead-end road, the estate became off limits to neighbors and the parents warned their kids to stay away. The warnings fell upon deaf ears for some of the kids and it became a challenge, especially around Halloween to sneak on and off the property without getting caught. The tragedy of Penny Myers ruined the once vibrant estate and changed the future of the Murphy family forever.

CHAPTER 2

Dirk was having a difficult time taking in everything he saw and just like Jerry, in the beginning was a little skeptical. A magical place basically in their own back yard? They had grown up here, had played in those pastures and swam in the bayou so many times they couldn't count. Why now? Why here? Places like this were on TV and never really existed. They both had questions gnawing at them, but neither of them were going to admit it.

Dirk was always the smarter of the two of them book wise, but where Jerry seemed to lack in school work, he made up tenfold in common sense and survival. He accredited his outdoor skills to having so many older siblings who had challenged him every day. It wasn't uncommon for his three older brothers to give him an hour head start to go hide in the woods. If they found him, they would torture him with a red belly or a quick suspension from a tree by his underwear. It wasn't a deliberate bout of meanness in their opinion, just a way to toughen up the spoiled brat.

Jerry became very good at ultimate hide and seek, as they called it and many times, Dirk would join them in the game. Sometimes they would find them, but most times they would not. They would usually give up after a couple of hours of frustrated searching and then start calling his name to surrender. Jerry would pop out of a hollow tree stump at times or crawl out from under the pile of leaves he had built and took pleasure in boasting all the way home.

The one spot that he never revealed was a place he built in the muddy bank of the bayou. The tide on the Intracoastal Canal had a swing of about four feet. At low tide, the water receded and left about a seven-foot-tall mud and clay mixture bank that was easy to dig. When the tide was out Jerry dug a hole into the bank about four feet in and then dug upwards about two feet leaving a space just big enough for them to sit in. When it was high tide his older brothers would chase them into the bayou and they would swim underwater into the hiding place and waited as they walked over the ground above. The hardest part of hiding here was trying to contain their laughter as they listened to them cuss each other when they couldn't find them. This magic place lasted for a few years and then finally eroded away with years of abuse from passing tug boats.

As Dirk and Jerry walked along the edge of the bayou towards the swamp and the other secret Jerry was talking about, they reminisced about the magic hiding spot and the great times they had there. That spot took a back seat to what lay before them now. This whole place was magical and there was no way anyone would find them here. It wasn't long before the questions from Dirk started up again.

"Where are we going?"

"I want to show you something!" Jerry said as he jumped over a rotten tree that had fallen over the path.

"Is it the girl? Asked Dirk.

"Maybe"

"Are you sure we're safe in the trees?"

"Yes, trust me. I have tried to bring all kinds of things into here, it doesn't work in the trees."

"Why?" Dirk asked.

"I don't know! I think the trees are kind of like a safe place. Everything I've tried out there in the pasture disappears as soon as I'm in the trees and trust me, I've thought of some crazy things."

"Like what?" Dirk was more curious.

"Well, I started with smaller things like a tiger and elephants and then I wanted to try something a little bigger. I took two steps into the pasture one day, thought of it, then said it." Jerry said as he stopped and turned towards Dirk on the trail

"Said what?" Dirk asked and swallowed hard.

"T-Rex!" Jerry boasted and smiled crazily.

"What? Have you lost your mind? What happened?"

Jerry continued down the trail towards the swamp with Dirk close behind listening intently.

"Like I said, I was only two steps out of the trees and I heard it, but I couldn't see it. I wanted to get a closer look so I walked out about 30 yards and there it was. It was the most amazing creature I'd ever seen and the scariest. The movies and the crap we learned in school about them was a joke." Jerry continued to speak.

"I watched it for about an hour and studied its movements, then I had to leave. I walked back to the trees and just like everything else, it was gone. I didn't want to be here alone after dark. I'm not too sure what goes on here after dark." Jerry explained and seemed to be concerned about the nights.

"What do you think happens here at night?" Dirk was curious now.

"I'm not sure, but that's why I brought you. I need you to stay with me one night and I'm pretty sure we will be safe in the trees." Jerry explained and faced Dirk.

"Pretty sure? You don't sound so sure." Dirk said and punched him in the arm. A term of endearment they often shared.

"We can tell our parents we are camping out next Saturday night." Jerry explained.

"As long as we are home Sunday morning. We both have to serve mass on Sunday at 10:00, remember?" Dirk reminded him.

The two of them had been altar boys at the St. Ann's Catholic Church since their first communion and rarely missed Sunday Mass.   Their parents were pretty understanding and allowed them to do a lot of things, but attending church and fulfilling their obligations as altar boys was a priority.

"So, what do ya say, will you stay in here with me Saturday night?" Jerry asked this time.

"I guess, if my parents say I can." Dirk answered.

They continued walking down the trail which turned and headed away from the bayou and towards a thick line of huge cypress trees. Thick moss hung down from some of the lower branches and the boys jumped at them, pulling some down. The sun was getting lower in the sky and Dirk was feeling a little uneasy. He knew he had to be home before dark and it was going to be a long walk back. He was also getting hungry and nagged at Jerry a little.

"Are we almost there? Dirk asked.

"Shh." Jerry said and told Dirk to get down. They both stooped low to the ground and ran to a nearby cypress tree. The boys took a knee behind it and leaned over to get a look.

"What is it?" Dirk whispered.

"It's her!" Jerry said and pulled a sling shot and ball bearings from his back pack.

@@@@@

"Sir, sir?" The flight attendant repeated and startled Dirk, who was still staring out the window deep in thought. He looked up from his seat and realized he was the last person on the plane. Embarrassed, he jumped up and reached for his carry on that was still tucked away in the compartment above his head. He exited the plane and made his way to baggage to pick up his only checked bag. Dirk powered his phone back up while he walked and it immediately blew up with text alerts. He scrolled through his phone and smiled. Jerry was outside the airport circling the arrival pick up lanes and was already giving Dirk a hard time.

If you need help in there with your five bags sweetheart, let me know? LOL!! Jerry texted.

Wouldn't want you to hurt your back old man, you better stay in the car. Dirk answered.

Dirk retrieved his bag, showed the attendant his matching ticket and stepped out into the warm humid air of South Louisiana. He had been in Florida now for 25 years and although the weather was similar, the humidity here was much worse. Jerry blew the horn at Dirk and positioned his car into a temporary parking spot for loading. Dirk dropped his bag near the back of the car and two of them briefly embraced.

"How the heck are you, man?" Dirk asked as he took a good look at his childhood friend.

"I'm better than you, buddy. At least I still have hair."

"You call that hair? I've seen better looking hair on salt meat!" They both laughed as they were interrupted by an officer telling them to move along. Jerry maneuvered through the traffic out of the airport and headed South on Airline highway towards 310 and Houma.

The two of them caught up on family and friends for the first 30 minutes and then stopped for a drink at a restaurant, well known for the best Bloody Mary's in the area. Jerry ordered two of them and they sat on the back patio overlooking the bayou. There was an awkward pause in the conversation until Dirk broke the silence.

"Do you ever think about her?"

"All the time!" Jerry answered without looking up, then took a long sip of his Bloody Mary.

CHAPTER 3

Dirk Matherne, one of three sons to Barbara and Kenneth Matherne and best friend to Jerry Davis also loved the outdoors. Playing sports meant everything to him and of course like most kids had aspirations of playing college and professional football. He was good at it and the team he and Jerry had played for was the best in the parish. The move from Pop Warner to the Junior High School football team had Dirk a little nervous at first, but he accepted the challenge and it was going well. Their team was already 2-0 and the coach was giving him plenty of playing time. Because of his size, he was moved from his position of safety to linebacker and he was learning fast.

Dirk was always a little bigger than the kids his age and his Dad pushed him to work on his speed. Playing in the shadows of his Dad who was the High School star wasn't always easy, but he took his advice whenever he could get it. One of the training devices he made for Dirk was a huge truck tire that he attached to a rope and harness and he would drag it around the yard. His speed was improving and the chances of playing on the 9th grade team were getting better as well. His games were played on Thursday afternoons while most of the parents were at work, but even in the absence of his Dad, he practiced and played hard to prove his worth.

@@@@@

"What are you doing?" Dirk asked as he watched Jerry load a ball bearing into the strap on his sling shot.

"Watch." He told Dirk as he took aim from behind the cypress tree and stretched the bands as far as he could.

Jerry released the leather strap and the ball bearing headed straight at the little girl's head.

She stood at the edge of the swamp next to a very large cypress stump with her back to them. Her long wavy blonde hair hung down low to her waist and a wreath of fresh flowers sat gracefully on top of her head. Her skin was slightly tanned and she appeared to be just over five feet tall with a slender build. She was barefoot, wearing shorts and a tank top with some iron on patch of a rock band.

Dirk watched the ball bearing in flight for a split second and then dove down behind the tree.

"Holy crap! Did you hit her?" Dirk whispered, untied his hoody and quickly pulled it over his head.

"I told you to watch!" Jerry said. "Now get up and look."

Dirk gathered himself, took a knee and poked his head around the tree to take a look. He watched in amazement as the ball bearing sat suspended in the air spinning just in front of the little girls' face. She had turned to face them and watched it closely, turning her head to the side like she was analyzing it. She smiled, raised her hand just below it, blinked her eyes once and it dropped into her palm.

"Welcome back Jerry." The girl giggled and seemed happy to see him.

Jerry grabbed his back pack off the ground, rolled his eyes at Dirk and started in the direction of the girl.

"It's good to be back" Jerry said as he approached her.

"I see you brought him this time?" The girl said as she lifted her eyes towards Dirk.

"Yes, I did. Just waiting on the right time, ya know?"

She smiled and offered her hand to Dirk when he finally made his way over.

"Hi, I'm Penny, Penny…"

"Myers." Dirk interrupted.

She laughed hard and took Dirk's hand in hers, but didn't shake it. She held on to it gently and surveyed his eyes like she was looking through him. Her eyes were a color of green Dirk couldn't describe. He stared back at her with an uneasy look and felt something very peculiar. Her hand was warm and her touch was inviting.

"You were right Jerry, he is nice." She said and pulled Dirk in the direction of the stump.

Dirk pulled back a little and gave Jerry an, *I'm going to kill you* look. Jerry smiled, gave him a reassuring head nod to follow her and he fell in right behind them. She led Dirk around to the other side of the stump and Dirk stopped in his tracks and jerked his hand back when he saw it.

@@@@@

Brenda Davis stood on the porch with a broom in her hands sweeping dirt and leaves off the front porch and straightening the black wrought iron chairs that sat around a small table. She wore a food stained apron over blue slacks, a white button up blouse and had removed her shoes. The sun was setting on another cool, fall day and the supper she had been working on all afternoon was almost ready. One of the kids was walking up the shell driveway from the neighborhood while some were staying with friends for the weekend. She loved having the rest of the kids at home together for dinner, but sometimes welcomed the break of a few being gone.

Saturdays in the neighborhood during football season held a tradition of its own. Families shared the burden of cooking for a large group and hosting one of the big college games. The game was usually preceded by a seafood boil and a game of touch football that always ended up being changed to full contact tackle. Jerry's mom wasn't worried he wasn't home yet, but just a little concerned because he was usually the one organizing the teams. As Jerry's older brother Mark stepped onto the porch sweaty and covered in dirt, she asked him about Jerry.

"Have you seen your little brother?"

"He left earlier with his girlfriend, Dirk". He said laughing and continued. "I saw them walking towards the woods."

"Yes, they said they were going for a walk, but would be back by supper." She said with a wrinkled brow.

"They're probably playing kiss chase." Mark added another insult.

"Oh, stop it!" She said and swatted at his butt with the broom. "Go get a bath, dinner is almost ready."

Mark picked up the pace to avoid the broom and slipped through the front screen door. Brenda Davis leaned the broom against the wall and noticed the streetlights flickering on one by one. The only sounds were the mating calls of distant cicadas and the grunt of a nearby bullfrog. She cupped her hands together around her mouth and called Jerry's name. Her voice echoed through the darkness and faded away at the end of the street. After a few calls from the porch, she could hear the phone ringing in the kitchen and hurried to answer it.

"Hey Brenda, it's Barbara. Have you seen the boys?"

"Not since they left at lunch. They said they were going for a walk in the woods, but would be back by supper. I'm sure they'll turn up soon. You know how those two are."

"Yes, I do and I'm sure you're right. Can you let me know when they return? Kenny wants him home before the game starts." Barbara stressed.

"I sure will!" Brenda assured.

They exchanged some pleasantries and before hanging up, promised to get together soon for coffee.

CHAPTER 4

The cypress stump that Dirk was staring at rose from the swamp about seven feet and was accompanied by three or four more stumps not quite as big. He had never seen one this big. The cypress tree that they surrounded was at least forty feet tall and covered with thick, long strands of grey Spanish moss. A few of the branches hung low and the moss seemed to drip off them like wax into the swampy water. Dirk moved in closer, noticed an opening in the stump that appeared to have stairs leading below ground and a light shimmered out onto the edges of the stump. Penny offered her hand again and asked if they wanted to go inside.

"Uh, no I don't think so!" Dirk stuttered as he stepped back.

"It's okay." Penny said. "It's totally safe." her sparkling green eyes looked through him again and Dirk instantly looked at his watch trying to avoid her mesmerizing gaze.

"I have to go!" He said. "My mom is expecting me." Dirk started walking towards the path that they had taken into the swamp and Jerry grabbed his arm.

"Hey, we don't wanna be rude!" He said holding on a little too tight for Dirk's taste.

"Let me go, Jerry. I have to go!" Dirk said a little more strongly.

"It's okay Jerry, let him go. Maybe he'll be ready next time?" Penny placed her hand on Dirk's shoulder. Within seconds that same peculiar feeling rushed through his body again and he felt warm all over.

"Yes, maybe next time." Dirk said smiling.

The boys said goodbye to Penny and started the long walk home. The sun was dropping behind the woods and long shadows from the cypress trees danced across the tall rye grass of the pasture.

There wasn't a lot of conversation on the walk back to the fence and Jerry didn't want to push the issue. He knew Dirk well enough to know when it was time to give him some space. When they arrived at the fence, Dirk turned to look back at the pasture and the silhouette of the cypress trees beyond the pasture faded into a blur of darkness.

"Do you think she realizes she's dead?" Dirk asked.

"I don't know, but she sure doesn't act like it bothers her if she does." Jerry answered.

"Well if she isn't dead, then what is she?" Dirk added.

"I'm not sure, but I wanna find out."

"This place is pretty cool!" Dirk said smiling at Jerry.

Jerry placed his muddy toes on the bottom wire and lifted the top one as well while Dirk squeezed through the barbed wire.

"Does that mean we are camping out next Saturday?" Jerry asked as he came through the fence. Dirk stood facing the fence and looked at the barn on the other side with a little more belief than before.

"I'll bring the hot dogs" Dirk said as he punched Jerry in the arm.

"Remember, not a word to anyone and you pinky swore." Jerry reminded.

"I know, I won't say a word to anyone."

The boys walked the fence line that bordered the Murphy's property and started running when they heard Jerry's mom calling his name. They busted through the back gate laughing and Red was there to greet them as usual. He followed the boys around to the front porch where Mrs. Davis waited with folded arms. A look that Jerry had seen many times before and he knew what it meant. Red found his favorite spot under the porch and resumed chewing on an old dirty bone.

"Wash your feet and get your butt in the house young man, you are late for supper!" Mrs. Davis ordered.

"Dirk, your mom said to hurry on home as well. I'll call her and let her know you're on the way."

"Yes ma'am" He said and broke out into a barefooted sprint down the street towards his house.

@@@@@@

Jerry quietly entered the door of the sacristy at St. Ann Church and found Dirk already robed up and preparing the offerings. He walked over to one of the lockers, found his robe and belt and was dressed in minutes. The two of them greeted Father Faucier and discussed a game plan for the service.

"Are you ringing the bells?" Dirk asked.

"I can if you want me to." Jerry said as he grabbed the candle lighter.

Dirk grabbed the six-foot sacred cross from its stand and the two of them led the priest outside to the front of the church. People were still filing in through the doors as the ushers scurried back and forth to find empty seats for them. They dipped their fingers in the holy water, followed by the sign of the cross at the church entrance and waited for a hand gesture from one of the ushers.

The choir broke into an entry hymn of Amazing Grace and the congregation stood as Father Faucier and the boys made their way to the altar. The boys split to each side of the altar and while Jerry lit the altar candles, Dirk helped prepare the hosts for communion. Father Faucier spoke from the bible about the commandments and stressed not coveting thy neighbor's goods.

The church was packed with people and the 10:00 AM service seemed to be the most popular. The Matherne family sat in their usual spot five pews back from the front, while the Davis' took up an entire pew for themselves. The older Davis kids with their wives and grandkids still felt the pressure from their mother to be there every Sunday and to sit together as a family. Brenda Davis listened to the message and beamed with pride as she held onto the arm of her husband cleansing her soul of impurities.

Jerry and Dirk went through the motions they had done so many times before, but their thoughts had drifted to another place. The next week at school would drag on as they anticipated their plans for the following Saturday. They thought of their secret world and Dirk had more questions that he needed answered. The waiting was eating him alive and he couldn't get the thought of Penny Myers out of his mind. He thought she was beautiful, but mysterious, scary and inviting at the same time. He felt strange about wanting to see her so badly and didn't understand why. Dirk would hide these feelings from Jerry, for now, to avoid any ridicule and hoped to understand a little better on Saturday, but that was an eternity away.

CHAPTER 5

Just as they thought, the week crawled by like a snail crossing over a gravel road, but it was Friday now and they were extremely excited about tomorrow. They both attended the local Friday night Varsity High School football game, after winning their JV game and made more plans for the camp out from the highest part of the bleachers.

Dirk was asking Jerry about supplies and food when he noticed he wasn't paying attention.

"Did you hear anything I just said" Dirk asked.

"What? Yes, I heard you." Jerry had a strange look on his face and Dirk knew he was lying. He followed Jerry's gaze and saw the distraction. Shannon Einstein, the girl of his dreams was standing against the rail watching the cheerleaders and Jerry was transfixed. Dirk punched him in the arm and the barrage of taunting commenced.

"Somebody's in love!" Dirk said laughing.

"I am not!" Jerry swung back and missed.

"Why don't you just go talk to her?"

"No way." Girls like that don't talk to guys like me." Jerry said still staring at her.

"Whatever, dude. Just go talk to her! Dirk pushed.

"She's talking to all of her friends, that's a death trap." Jerry said and redirected his interest to the game as the crowd jumped to their feet cheering. Jerry stood and admired the receiver handing the ball over to the referee after scoring a touchdown.

"That's gonna be me out there."

"That's hopefully gonna be both of us one day." Dirk added as they took a seat. "If I wouldn't have broken my leg at the beginning of the season, I'd be out there playing right now."

"Yeah, yeah, can we get on with the plans now?" Dirk pleaded.

"Sure!" Jerry answered as he sipped his coke.

The two of them discussed food items, drinks and what camping gear they may need. The plan was to meet at Jerry's house in the afternoon to gather supplies and be at the fence by 3 PM. This would give them time to cross over and be in the trees to set up well before dark.

@@@@@

Saturday afternoon the boys met as planned and borrowed Dirk's older brother's two-man tent. They stuffed snacks, hotdogs and drinks into two backpacks. Jerry grabbed a lighter from his mom's purse and was tempted to grab a few cigarettes, but changed his mind when his older brother Mark came in.

"What are you stealing brat?" Mark asked when he saw Jerry pull his hand from the purse.

"Nothing." Jerry said leaving the room.

"I heard you and your girlfriend are going camping tonight?" Mark continued to ridicule. "You better watch out for the ghost out there!"

Jerry stopped at the door.

"What are you talking about?" Jerry was curious.

"Rumor has it that the ghost of Penny Myers is back there and she likes to drown people." Mark said smirking and waited for a response.

"Whatever!" Jerry responded nervously and ran to the front room where Dirk was waiting.

"Come on, let's get out of here" Jerry said as he grabbed his backpack and headed out of the door. Dirk followed as did Red when he saw them step off the porch and head for the back gate. The boys exited the back yard as Mark watched them from the back-bedroom window and laughed aloud when he thought of the plans he had for them tonight.

@@@@@

Summer 1976

Penny Myers had visited her Uncle Murphy many times before so she was excited about returning. She would miss four days of school, but being an honor roll student, they knew she would be okay. Her parents were pioneering a new line of natural foods and while excited about broadening the business overseas to Paris, they couldn't afford to take Penny along.

They lived an hour west of Bourg in the slightly bigger town of Lafayette and the only family they trusted to leave her with were the Murphy's. Penny had an aunt in the area, but she was not capable of taking care of herself, much less a young girl for a week.

They dropped her off on route to the New Orleans airport and Penny was out of the car running towards the stables before they came to a stop. She loved horses and her Uncle Murphy had plenty to go around. Her favorite was a five-year-old Paint named Max. Before her parents pulled away from the farm, she was already in the saddle riding circles in the training pen. Michael watched from the fence and would laugh and clap every time she made another round. Penny's mom watched from the car window at her daughter smiling and waving while she rode Max in circles and was cautiously worried about leaving her daughter here for a week.

Penny rode Max around the pen for a while until her Uncle Murphy showed up and was saddled in on his own horse.

"You done messing around?" He asked as he held the reins and looked like he had just stepped out of a country western movie. He wore Wrangler jeans topped with leather chaps, a shiny buttoned long sleeve shirt and a huge cowboy hat. "What do you say, should we take them out for a run?"

Penny was about to come out of her skin with excitement.

"Yes!" She squealed and led Max over to the gate. One of the hired hands opened the gate and Max pranced out of the pen like he was on parade.

"We'll keep it slow at first, then we can pick it up on the other side of the pasture." Uncle Murphy instructed.

"Yes sir!" Penny said.

They started out to the pasture with a trot and Michael started clapping and ran behind them until he was corrected by the hired hand. He stopped running, watched them enter the pasture and then stomped over to the barn like a man on a mission. He returned shortly straddling a mop that had a rope attached and rode it back and forth through the yard smiling from ear to ear.

Uncle Murphy and Penny rode the horses for a couple of hours and pulled back into the stables just before dark. Penny was tired and her uncle could tell in her riding. She sat lower in the saddle and he noticed her boots slipping from the stirrups. As she neared the gate, one of the dogs bolted out from behind the fence and nipped at Max's hind leg, startling him and causing him to rare up. Penny lost her footing in the stirrups and the reins were snatched from her hands. She tried to recover, but fell backwards onto the ground and struck her head hard on the dirt. Darkness overcame her and within seconds her Uncle Jack was at her side. He hovered over the top of her as a worker quickly grabbed the reigns of Max and ushered him to the stable.

"Penny, are you okay?" He asked giving her a gentle shake.

Her eyes squinted open and she could see a shape above her. Uncle Jack wiped the dust from her forehead.

"Are you okay, Penny?" He asked again.

"Yes sir, I'm fine, but I have a headache."

"You took a pretty good fall. Are you sure?"

"Yes sir, I'm fine!" Penny assured him and she sat up.

"Okay, let's get you up and get ready for dinner." Jack helped her up and walked her over to the stable. He explained to her that it was important to have contact with Max after the incident. It was a psyche thing to reunite the rider with the horse to calm both of them. Horses can sense fear, Jack explained and he didn't want Penny scared after the unfortunate accident. She walked over to the gate and cautiously put her hand through.

"It's okay boy. I know you didn't mean it." Penny offered in a soft tone.

Max walked over to the gate and sniffed the back of her hand and then allowed her to rub his nose.

"There you go. No love lost and y'all can pick up where you left off tomorrow." Jack said as he threw some fresh hay over the gate. Jack and Penny left the barn and headed inside to wash up for dinner as the workers prepared the horses for the evening. Penny walked onto the porch and felt a little nauseated, but it seemed to fade away as she entered the house.

Michael was already seated at the table eating as Mrs. Murphy set the table for the rest of them. He was on a strict schedule and any variation from that schedule would send him into a fit of rage. Feeding times and medication amounts were a calculated necessity and Mrs. Murphy had it down to a science.

They all met back at the table and enjoyed catching up on school, family and the workings of a farm. Penny was given her schedule for the week and was happy to help out, knowing there would be some more riding involved. After supper, they moved to the front porch where Mrs. Murphy read some poetry to the three of them. It was Michael's favorite part of the day and the rhyming words seemed to calm him the most before bed.

The night sky was clear, showing off an array of bright stars against a jet-black background. The temperature was dropping some and the cool clean air set the stage for a perfect summer evening. They enjoyed the sounds of the crickets for a while and then turned in to bed early. Penny had trouble sleeping thinking about the exciting week that was in store for her. Her head started to hurt again from the fall and nausea soon overcame her. Penny jumped from the bed and just made it to the toilet before she vomited. She could feel her heartbeat crashing on both sides of her head. She wanted to tell her uncle about the pain, but didn't want to bother him so late. Soon the dizziness was too much. She wiped her mouth with a wet towel, laid her face on the cool hard floor and fell asleep.

CHAPTER 6

The next two days went by in a blink for Penny as the chores were completed and the riding continued. She was getting better every day and seriously thought about becoming a rider in competition. She had always loved horses and felt very comfortable with them.

"If you're serious I'll talk to your Dad about spending summers here." Uncle Jack offered. "I can have Joe work with you. He was one of the best in the state in calf roping, but also taught barrel racing to some of the top females."

"Are you serious? That would be awesome!" Penny gleamed.

"Okay, I'll talk to him this weekend when they return. Why don't you take the rest of the day off and go explore the back pastures? It's beautiful back there. I'm good friends with the owners and I'm sure they won't mind. Just be careful near the water and be back before supper."

"Yes sir, sounds like fun!" Penny said as she dusted her hands off on the back of her shorts. Her tank top that was adorned with her favorite band Dr. Hook was splattered with mud from a hard morning of chores.

Penny grabbed a quick drink from the water hose and headed down the fence line to the Thompson's property. She stopped at a corner where the fences met and climbed over the horizontal wooden post that strengthened the fence at the corners. When she plopped down on the other side, her shoe sank into the mud and it came off when she lifted her foot.

"Oh great!" She mumbled as she balanced on one foot trying not to get her sock muddy as well. She bent over, pulled her shoe out and quickly put it on before she fell over. Finding some harder land near the grass, she leaped and landed right on the edge. The sound of clapping came from behind her and she was surprised to see that Michael had followed her to the fence. She had no idea he was there.

"You're muddy!" He said smiling, pointing to her shoe and then repeated it twice.

"That's okay, it'll wash off." She said. "You better go on back to the farm Michael, your mom will be worried." Penny stressed.

"Okay, okay, okay" Michael repeated and left in the direction of the farm.

Penny watched him for a minute and then followed the dirt road to the cattle guard. She carefully stepped across the metal grates and then found a grassy path through the pasture leading to the Intracoastal Canal. She had swum there a few summers ago with her parents, but had never been back here alone. She felt slightly liberated and felt the urge to sing out loud as she walked. Besides, nobody would hear her this far back, well, maybe the cows she thought. Penny sang her favorite Dr. Hook song softly as she walked the path that led her to the water. She stopped at the tree line and looked back to see if she was still alone. The pasture was empty except for a few cows and a large white bird riding on the back of one. They chewed the grass as they walked and with little effort, swung their tails back and forth to swat the flies. They paid no attention to her as she scanned the area for any company. She walked a little further into the trees and found the swimming hole she had been to before in a little cove off the main canal. When she was sure no one was around, she found a downed tree, stripped down to her panties and bra and jumped off the muddy bank into the water.

The water was colder than she expected and it took her breath away at first. She surfaced and screamed, splashing the water with her arms in an attempt to warm herself. It didn't take long for her body to adjust and she swam around enjoying the peace and quiet. Penny was a great swimmer and felt very confident in her underwater capabilities. Her Dad often joked that she had gills.

In the middle of the cove was a small platform that some local boys had built to climb up and jump off. Penny had jumped from it before and felt sure she could do it again. It was about ten feet off the water at the top and she scaled up the make shift ladder easily. She looked down at the water below and was about to jump when something caught her eye. She looked over to the tree where her clothes were laying and she saw him. Michael was sitting on the tree with her clothes in his hand screaming something inappropriate. She instantly tried to cover her bra and panties with both arms as best as she could, but then lost her footing. Penny fell backwards from the top and hit her head against a large plank on the way down, knocking her unconscious. Her limp body splashed into the water on the other side of the platform and she slowly sank to the bottom.

@@@@@

Dirk and Jerry rocked back and forth and continued to catch up on old times while enjoying their second Bloody Mary. It was like they never missed a step. The friendship that the two of them shared was like no other. Being apart for so many years had led them in different directions, but they always seem to pick right back up where they left off.

"Do you ever wish we could go back again?" Dirk asked.

"Of course, I do." Jerry said as he watched an alligator appear on the surface of the water on the other side of the bayou. "There's not a day goes by that I don't think about that time. The decisions we made that day changed everything. Still so hard to believe."

Dirk's cell phone chirped with a new message and he slid it from his pocket. He read the message, put it back in his pocket and finished the last sip of his drink.

"You mind if we get going, I don't wanna be late for our meeting?" Dirk asked.

"No not at all, I'll pay the tab and meet you back here in a minute." Jerry said as he got up from his chair. "I don't wanna be late either."

Dirk rose from his chair, gazed at the water and watched the alligator again as it moved effortlessly through the bayou and then disappeared under the black murky water. The familiar hum of a tugboat engine caught his attention and he watched as one approached from the West. His mind drifted again and he remembered.

— — — — — —

"Are you sure the workers are gone?" Dirk asked.

"Yes, I saw the last guy leave 30 minutes ago and the security guard won't be here until 10:00 o'clock. We have a few hours, come on." Jerry grabbed Dirk's hand as he leaped from the land onto the tug boat. The night was dark except for a few street lights burning near the old ferry. The wooden docks and ramps were still in place, but the ferry was decommissioned in the early 70's when the bridge was put in. Many locals used it as a makeshift boat ramp, but it mostly served as a fishing spot for the nearby kids. Jerry turned the lever of a heavy outer door and struggled to open it until Dirk helped. The smell of fresh paint poured out of the compartment as they stepped inside.

The boat belonged to RAYCO Inc., one of the three boat and barge fabrication companies that surrounded the neighborhood. This boat was still in the early phase, lacked a motor, electronics and was a shell of steel and lead paint. It was a dangerous lure for young boys wanting to explore, but a great diving platform into the muddy waters of the Intracoastal Canal.

Once inside, Jerry turned on his flashlight and they took some stairs leading down to the empty engine room. They climbed around and swung from pipes for a while and then headed up to the bridge. The large windows that adorned the front of the boat were free of glass at this point. Jerry and Dirk took their places behind the console and went to work as the Captain and First Mate.

"Are all the lines in?" The Captain asked.

"Aye, sir and the crew is looking forward to the trip."

"Very good, then. Give me 1/2 throttle until we are clear of the dock."

"Aye, sir!"

The boys stared out into the dark night and navigated the large boat meticulously through the Intracoastal and over to the Gulf of Mexico. They had adventures of giant squids attacking the boat and a fire on the back deck that was quickly extinguished by the crew. They were just about to catch a whale when they heard Dirk's mom yell his name from the front porch.

"Dirk!" Dirk, you ready?" Jerry said standing at the back door of the restaurant.

Torn away from his thoughts again, Dirk joined Jerry at the door and they navigated through the busy restaurant to the car. The two of them followed highway 90 into Houma and parked in the parking lot of Thibodeaux and Webb, Attorneys at Law, thirty minutes early. They situated themselves away from the building and didn't want to seem too eager for the appointment. They rolled the windows down and enjoyed the cool breeze that always seemed to follow a good thunderstorm. Jerry left the radio on low, tuned into his favorite 80's songs and attempted to sing along with his own version of AC/DC.

"I can see you're still stuck in the 80's and all the money you made didn't go to singing lessons." Dirk joked.

"You just don't appreciate good singing when you hear it." Jerry added and continued to butcher *Back in Black*.

Dirk watched the front door of the office, felt a little anxious and his tone changed.

"Who do you think it is?"

"I'm not sure, but it better be worth it."

The words no sooner left Jerry's mouth when a large black SUV pulled into the parking lot and took up a space right in front of the door of the attorney's office.

"We have company!" Dirk spoke in a softened, but excited voice.

"Yep, it sure looks that way!" Jerry said as they both were fixated on the passenger door.

A very large man dressed in a black suit circled around the back of the SUV, surveyed the area briefly and opened the rear passenger door.

Dirk was the first to notice the high heeled shoe and the long, tanned legs extend out from the opened door.

"Whoa, who the hell is that? He said, mesmerized at the tall slender woman stepping out of the car.

"I'm not sure? Maybe it's another client for a different case or something?" Jerry was guessing.

She had a solemn look on her face that was somewhat shielded by a large black hat. Her tight black dress was cut short, about mid-thigh, and her legs appeared strong and toned. She looked to be in her mid to late 30's and very well put together by Dirk and Jerry's standards. They both sat there speechless and watched her walk into the front door as the large man held it for her and then stood outside facing the SUV. Through his sunglasses, the man peered in their direction and the two of them sunk in their seats a bit.

"Oh crap, we're busted! He's looking right at us!" Jerry said laughing and swung his hand over to hit Dirk in the upper arm.

"Well, you were gawking at her like a buzzard over road kill!" Dirk added.

"Oh, and you weren't?" Jerry teased.

"Hey, I know it's a sore subject, but have you heard from Mark." Dirk asked.

The mood in the car changed quickly after the question as Dirk patiently waited for an answer.

"No and I'm not expecting to either." Jerry answered gripping the steering wheel a little tighter. "Haven't seen or heard from him in over 20 years."

"That's so weird!" Dirk added.

"Yea, tell me about it. The only one in the family to take off and not a word from him. He graduated, joined the Marines and fell off the face of the earth." Jerry continued. "We tried to locate him after we found out he was back from a brief tour in Desert Storm, but didn't have any luck. I guess some people just want to live their life like that?"

"I guess." Dirk acknowledged.

The two of them shook their heads in unison and then carried on some more about old memories and of course, Penny Myers.

CHAPTER 7

Michael watched in silence with wide eyes as Penny fell from the platform, hit her head and splashed into the water. He stood quickly and clapped his hands vigorously as if to applaud her performance. Her clothes fell from his hands and he continued to clap, waiting for her to surface. After a few minutes of waiting, Michael became nervous and started to pace back and forth along the bank. Finally fear overcame him and he entered the water calling her name wildly. He thrashed about in waste deep water and wanted to go deeper, but he couldn't. Even in his state, he knew his limitations and he was not a good swimmer. He screamed her name over and over, became more frustrated and then started to hit himself in the face. He continued to do this for a minute and then returned to the tree where he was sitting.

He sat there with his hands over his face, looking through opened fingers at times, like a child playing peek-a-boo and watched a tugboat and barge passing in the canal. The barge was loaded with heavy equipment and the weight of it was displacing the water in the canal. The kids would call this type of barge a sucking barge, because it would pull the water away from the banks and take anything loose with it. Most parents watching their kids swim in the bayou, knew of this and would make them stay close to the bank until the barge passed and it was safe.

The water that was surrounding the platform was now sucked out to the middle of the canal while the boat passed. As soon as it was gone, with a wave similar to a small tsunami, the water rushed back into the cove and sloshed around forming a muddy water pit full of debris. Michael wept loudly and sat there frozen until darkness started to envelope the woods. He looked at her clothes on the ground, picked them up and smelled them. He used them to wipe the tears from his face and jumped when he heard a voice behind him.

"What are you doing back here Michael?" A familiar voice asked from the edge of the trees.

@@@@@

Penny woke and felt her body being pushed and pulled with her excruciating headache increasing with the slightest movement. Confusion and panic began to set in as she tried to figure out where she was. Her eyes burned as she opened and closed them and could see nothing but a yellow haze through the muddy water. She couldn't tell which way was up and she started to gasp.

Water, she thought. *I'm underwater.* Hold your breath, she told herself and she felt some force pulling her down and away. She tried to swim against it, but it was too strong and suddenly her body hit something. Penny was getting weaker and started to suck in some more water. Don't give up, she thought. With one more attempt to free herself she felt with her hands for anything to hold onto. She scratched at the bottom, but only fingered the soft mud beneath her and in a last-ditch effort, pushed herself up with her feet as hard as she could. Her upper torso flung out of the water and as she gasped for air, her head struck something hard. Through blurry eyes she tried to focus in the dark space and wasn't sure where she was. It took her a few seconds before she realized she was inside a small void of the platform.

Her head was cut in two places, one on the back and now a new one on top. Her scalp bled profusely and stained her shiny, wet, blonde hair. Tiny strips of light beamed through between the boards of the dark space and she pulled herself up to lay on the small planks of wood. She was feeling weak again and knew she didn't have much time. She tried putting pressure on the cuts with her hands, but it made no difference. She laid across the wood just above the water and pressed her face against the side boards to look through the crack. Still trying to catch her breath, she could partially see Michael standing on the bank with his hands over his eyes and one more person she didn't recognize. The cuts continued to bleed as she tried to cry for help, but there was no sound. Her lips parting and only whispering the words.

"Michael, help! Help me please!

@@@@@

Mark sat on the kitchen bar with his feet propped up on the back of a chair talking to his friend Duke on the phone. The long, curled cord dangled from the phone and made a huge loop that was attached to the receiver mounted on the wall. The round plastic rotary dial was filthy from years of use by the kid's dirty fingers.

"You want to have a little fun tonight?" Mark asked Duke over the phone.

"Sure, what do you wanna do?"

"My brother and his friend are camping out back on the Thompson's land. I think it's time they met the ghost of Penny Myers."

"Oh, that does sound like fun. What time are we leaving?"

"Well, they left a few hours ago so I say we wait until an hour after dark and then start heading that way." Mark explained.

"Sounds good, I'll be at your house at 8:00."

"Hey Duke, do you think you can borrow a dress from one of your sisters and bring it with you?" Marked asked.

"I'm sure I can find one in their closet. We're gonna scare the pants off them." Duke laughed.

"I know, but the spoiled brat deserves a little scare. See you later." Mark said and hung up the phone. Now, if I can just find that wig from Halloween, he thought.

CHAPTER 8

Jerry scanned the area to make sure they weren't being followed and stepped closer to their spot on the fence. He placed his backpack on the ground and stepped on the middle wire to push it down.

"Are you ready?" Jerry asked and held the fence for Dirk.

"I guess." Dirk said and stepped through.

Jerry took another look just to be safe and pushed the backpacks through to Dirk on the other side. He squeezed through the barbed wire to the other side too and found Dirk standing there staring at the sky.

"Amazing, isn't it?" Jerry said as he handed Dirk his pack and shouldered his own.

"Yes, it is." Dirk agreed. "It's still so hard to believe that this is here. It's been right under our noses all this time."

"Yep" Jerry agreed. "That's why we have to be careful not to be followed and to respect this place. I have a feeling it could all just go away just as fast as it got here."

"What do you mean?"

"I mean, this is all here for a reason and I don't think it's been here that long. I think we were brought to this place on purpose. I'm just not sure why?" Jerry explained.

"Well, maybe tonight we'll get some answers." Dirk said as he readjusted his back pack.

"I hope so. To be honest, I think it has a lot to do with Penny. Don't you think it's strange that she is the only person here? Jerry questioned.

"Yes, I do, but I think everything here is strange. Where else can you think of something, wish for it out loud and it appears?" Dirk agreed.

"Be careful, we're a long way from the trees." Jerry warned.

"Have you ever tried food?" Dirk asked as he carefully stepped on the cattle guard.

"Of course, but for some reason it doesn't work. The only thing I've noticed to work so far is animals." Jerry explained. "I've also noticed you can't take anything back across the fence. It vanishes as soon as you go through."

"Bummer, I was hoping to put a baby Raptor in your brother Mark's room." Dirk smirked.

"Now that would be funny!" Jerry agreed.

The boys talked of ideas, but were careful not to verbally request them as they continued their trek to the trees. They looked forward to seeing Penny again and get some answers to the multitude of questions they had for her.

Jerry crossed the cattle guard right behind Dirk and Dirk turned to ask another question.

"Have you been in the stump yet?"

"No, she hasn't invited me."

"Why not?"

"Not sure, maybe she didn't trust me yet? She sure seems to have taken a liking to you though." Jerry smiled.

"Whatever."

The camp site was just off the muddy bank of the canal in a clearing by the cove. The boys had camped there before, but only from the other side so it seemed a little strange. They set up the tent after some confusion and arguing, then stuffed their packs inside. They went on a quick hunt for some firewood and split up to save time. They started a wood stack near an old dead tree that had fallen years ago. Dirk stopped on the edge of the cove and looked at the old platform that he, Jerry and some of his older brothers had built. He noticed it should have been more weathered and falling apart by now, but it wasn't. It looked brand new like when they first built it. It was at one time a rite of passage to be able to swim in the cove. The older kids would not let you swim until you jumped off the top and he remembered his first time. He revisited the scene and visualized himself climbing up. Something about this place accentuated that vision in his head and he felt like he was there. His arms and legs felt weak as he climbed to the top. Ten feet seemed like a long way up. He picked a spot in the water that he felt was deep enough, closed his eyes and jumped. The cool water that surrounded him felt good on that hot summer day and he felt a huge sense of accomplishment when he surfaced and heard the cheers from the older siblings and friends. Dirk had overcome his fear of heights by believing in himself and welcomed the acceptance from his peers.

He snapped back to the magic place smiling and picked up a rock to skim across the water. Just like Jerry's, the rock kept skipping all the way to the other side of the canal which was over a hundred yards. A feat that he could never accomplish on the other side. He watched as the circular ripples on the surface of the water expanded outward and then disappeared into the banks of the cove.

Dirk gathered some more wood and returned to the campsite with an armful and placed them on the stack that Jerry had started. They unpacked some items from their back packs and situated their sleeping bags inside the tent. It was an hour before dark and they decided to head to the swamp to see Penny and planned to return to the campsite for the night.

They grabbed the flashlights, a couple of snacks and headed back down the trail towards the swamp. It wasn't long until they arrived at the cypress stump where Dirk had met Penny for the first time. Dirk walked around to the other side of the stump to see the opening, but it was covered with moss. He looked at Jerry, swallowed hard and slowly reached for the moss. Suddenly, a hand poked through from the other side and grabbed his wrist. Dirk jumped back and tripped on

another stump which made him fall to the ground. Jerry started laughing and walked over to him to lend a hand.

"Don't feel bad buddy, she did the same thing to me. Scared the crap out of me too!" Jerry said as he helped him to his feet. Penny stepped through the moss with a comforting smile on her face and offered an apology.

"I'm sorry Dirk!" She said staring at him with those eyes again. Dirk stared back and instantly forgave her. They both gazed at each other for an uncomfortable amount of time before Jerry spoke up and snapped his fingers in between their faces.

"Hey, you two love birds need some time alone? I can leave, you know." Jerry asked jokingly while throwing a thumb over his shoulder.

They both realized they were caught up in a moment and Dirk blushed and turned to Jerry.

"Don't be stupid." Dirk said embarrassed.

"Are you ready to see it now?" Penny wasted no time picking up where they left off and pointed towards the stump.

Dirk looked at Jerry for guidance and he answered with a shrugging of his shoulders.

"I guess so." Dirk answered unsure of the consequences.

Penny took his hand and led him to the top of the stairs that seemed to vanish into a bright light somewhere down below. Jerry followed close behind and although his gut told him something was very wrong with this, he couldn't resist.

CHAPTER 9

Mark and Duke were decked out in their camouflage hunting gear each yielding a flashlight and Mark also had a back pack. They followed the road to the end of the neighborhood towards the Murphy's place and snuck past the farm unnoticed. They knew old man Murphy would be asleep by now and any workers that were possibly still employed would have gone home hours ago. They passed by the abandoned training pen and barn, then jumped the fence near the back corner of the property. Mark lit up a cigarette and offered one to Duke who accepted it and did the same.

"Your Dad would kill you if he knew." Duke laughed.

"Yes, I know, but he ain't gonna know."

They kept the flashlights turned off as they walked, wanting to go unnoticed until the right moment.

Making their way through the pasture the two of them kept silent, other than the occasional giggle when thinking of what they were about to do. They moved slowly and stayed low when they approached the woods, but were surprised not to see the glow of a campfire by now. Mark motioned for Duke to stop and he slid the pack off his shoulder. He quietly unzipped it and pulled a long red dress and a wig from inside.

"Here, put this on! Mark whispered.

"What? No! I'm not putting that on. This was your idea, you put it on." Duke responded quietly through a tightened jaw.

Mark laughed quietly and slipped the red dress over his clothes and pulled the wig over his short, jet black hair.

"How do I look?" He said as he combed his long blonde hair with his fingers.

"I'd date ya." Duke answered covering his mouth concealing a hysterical laugh.

"Let's go."

Mark led the way down the trail and instructed Duke to stop short of the camp site and shine the light at him when he approached from the other side. Duke did as he was told, hid behind a tree and waited for Mark's signal. Mark circled the campsite from a distance in the trees and was still confused about not seeing a fire. He crept up closer to the site and listened for any signs or sounds of the campers. Mark stepped out from behind the tree and studied the campsite with his flashlight. Confusion set in and he shined the light over in Dukes direction to get his attention.

"I don't understand." Mark scratched his wig and then slowly slid it off.

Duke joined him in the camping area and had a look of confusion himself.

"Where are they?"

"I don't know, they said they were camping right here." Mark took the dress off and looked around for any signs of gear.

"Maybe they got scared and went home?" Duke added.

"No, that's not like Jerry. He loves it out here." Mark continued. "Something's not right. This is where he camps every time."

"Where else could they be?"

"I have no idea, but I'm gonna find out." Mark stuffed the dress and wig back into the pack and shouldered it. Then he shined his light out into the cove and it a reflected across the surface of the water. He raised the beam up a little and the light illumined the old platform in the middle of the cove. It was old and falling apart and pieces of it hung down from the top. For a long time after the accident, this place was off limits. For the first year, the Thompson's beefed up security and no one was allowed to come on the property, but the tragic memories of Penny Myers seemed to fade with time.

"Look at that!" Mark said. "The old platform we built. We used to have fun jumping off that thing."

"Yea, that's cool. I remember you telling me about it, but never got an invite." Duke stood behind him pointing his light at it and squinting to get a better look.

"You wouldn't have jumped." Mark teased.

"You're probably right. I still have a fear of heights."

"Come on, let's get out of here and go find them." Mark said and started for the trail. Duke stepped in front of him and led the way while Mark paused for a second and shined the light back behind him towards the cove. He shined his light at an old China ball tree next to the water and illuminated the ground near the bottom of it. He stood there for few moments and wondered if it was still buried there.

@@@@@

The light was blinding and the boys had to close their eyes while carefully stepping down the stairs. They both raised a hand to shield some of the light as they descended the stairs. Dirk held onto Penny's hand tightly and followed her lead when she slowed near a door at the bottom. She opened the door and they all stepped into a small room with a huge window on the other side. The glass in the window was nothing they had seen before. It was fluid like water and rippled on the surface with nothing recognizable on the other side.

The light dimmed a little in the room when Penny shut the door and the boys lowered their hands from their eyes. The two walls without the window were stark white and when Penny raised her hand to each one, they transformed into a beautiful landscape of the countryside with wild horses

72

running free. Curiosity was eating Dirk alive and he was the first to speak.

"What is this place?"

"It's the window room. I made it myself. Do you like it.?" Penny moved her arms gracefully as she manipulated the walls in different places and the colors changed with every touch.

"It's beautiful, but how? Dirk asked and was interrupted by Penny's sweet voice.

"She said I could stay here for a while until things were figured out. Let me show you!"

"She?" Jerry asked, leaning in closer.

"Yes, she. Not a voice, but a presence of a female." Penny answered.

Penny pointed to the window and the ripples started to form into a picture. Jerry and Dirk watched wide eyed as it focused into a perfect view of the cove on a bright sunny day. It was so clear and vivid, it felt like they were standing on the bank watching in real time.

The sun shimmered across the water in the cove while the trees in full bloom, swayed back and forth in the summer breeze. The surface of the water was interrupted as they watched Penny splash down after a jump from the bank. She was wearing only a bra and panties and screamed when she surfaced. The boys were a little uneasy and confused watching her swim in the cove half-dressed while simultaneously standing next to her in the room. She splashed the water with her arms enjoying the water and then swam towards the platform. They watched with anticipation as she climbed to the top and prepared herself for the jump. Stepping closer to the window, Dirk swallowed hard and focused on Penny when she suddenly screamed and tried covering herself with her arms. Instantly, the ripples in the window expanded and the picture went out of focus when they heard a voice call out for Jerry. It was the voice of Mark and he didn't sound pleased.

"Jerry!" Mark called out in an aggravated posture as he and Duke walked along the trail towards the swamp. They passed a row of cypress trees and moved the light beams back and forth across the path to ward off any critters. South Louisiana was well known for cotton mouth snakes and some good-sized gators, two reptiles of which they wanted nothing to do with tonight. Mark stopped at a large cypress stump swallowed up by the thick hanging moss and there was no answer.

"I don't think they're out here." Mark said, shining the light across the swamp into the blackness. The light exposed the fog that rose softly up from the water and he caught a glimpse of glowing eyes staring back at him.

"We've been duped!" Mark frowned.

"I agree! So, can we go home now?" Duke asked and shined the light directly into Mark's eyes.

Mark blocked some of the light with his hand and shot his light back at Duke. After a few minutes when the dueling light fight was over they decided to head back to the house. There would be no fun tonight and Mark couldn't wait to get home and tell his parents that Jerry had lied about camping. The spoiled brat would at least get punished and maybe even get a few swats from their Dad. Mark would bathe in the delight of seeing this for a long time.

CHAPTER 10

From the other side, inside the stump, Jerry and Dirk panicked when they heard Mark calling. Penny raised her hand and told them to relax. She walked over to the window and slid her hand over the ripples until a picture came into focus. They stared at the window as Mark and Duke came into full focus. They were amazed to see them standing just in front of them. Both boys took a step back and looked for the door to the stairs, but didn't find it.

"It's okay, they can't see or hear you." Penny reassured them.

"Are you sure?" Dirk whispered.

"CAN YOU HEAR ME?" Penny screamed loudly from the room and smiled when there was no reaction. They watched Mark and Duke jousting with the flashlights and then turn to head out of the woods. More confusion set in with the boys and Penny walked back over to the window.

"I need to show you more." Penny touched the fluid again and the ripples began to expand.

"I have to go!" Jerry said anxiously. "Come on Dirk." Jerry moved towards the place where he remembered the door being and Dirk followed with a look of concern.

"Wait, I really need to show you this!" Penny pleaded and placed her hand on Dirk's shoulder.

"I think we've seen enough for one night. Where is the door?" Jerry asked.

Penny moved in front of them and her eyes glowed green in the darkness of the room.

"If I let you go, do you promise to return? I really need you to see one more thing." She said in a soft sweet tone.

Jerry turned to Dirk and his eyebrows lowered when he spoke.

"Yes, we will both be back, we promise. Right Dirk?"

Dirk picked up on his best friend's sarcasm and would have agreed to anything at this point.

"Yes, of course.

"Okay, the door is here." Before the words finished coming from her mouth, the door and stairs appeared behind her as she stepped aside. The bright light was blinding again as they carefully made their way up and out of the stump. As they pushed through the thick moss covering the door, they were delighted when they saw the woods again and they ran like they were being chased. The boys quickly dismantled the tent and stuffed it into the backpack, then gathered the rest of the camping gear.

Time was not on their side with Mark going home to spill the beans to the parents so they wasted no time getting back to the fence. They crossed between the magic posts, ran over to the next section and crossed back onto the Thompson's property as quickly as possible. When they reached the cattle guard, they ducked behind a large roll of hay as Mark and Duke slowly passed by, telling jokes and laughing.

When it was clear, they made their way to the campsite, started a fire and pitched the tent. It was a lot easier this time because there was no argument. They were on a mission now and knew it was only a matter of time until one or both of their parents came looking for them.

Just as they expected, within an hour they could see a multitude of flashlights moving in all directions coming towards them in the woods. Jerry sat on an old tree stump with a marshmallow hanging off the end of a coat hanger, glowing red and blue from the fire while Dirk stood and stuffed the final bite of a hotdog into his mouth. They both acted a little shocked when Mark, Duke and both of their fathers rounded the corner of the trail and entered the campsite. The looks on Mark and Duke's faces were priceless and Jerry looked over and winked at Dirk. They held back a smile as the confused looks turned into a barrage of questions.

"Where were you guys?" Mark asked with an incriminating tone.

Jerry blew out the fire on his marshmallow as he pulled it close and had his own question.

"What do you mean?"

"You guys were not here an hour ago!" Mark said looking at Duke for agreement.

"He's right, y'all weren't here." Duke interjected.

"We've been right here all night," Dirk piped up addressing his Dad.

"Jerry, have y'all been here?" Jerry had heard this tone from his Dad many times before and in his mind, the answer would not be a lie.

"Yes Dad, honest. We have been right here all night. I'm not sure where they were looking, but it couldn't have been here." Jerry answered and looked right into his Dad's eyes.

"He's lying Dad!" Mark was quick to respond.

Mr. Davis leaned into his son Mark and gave him a subtle smack on the head.

"You drug me all the way out here away from my football game for nothing? I'm sorry Ken, my son is an idiot!" Mr. Davis said glaring at Mark.

"It's alright, I'm just glad they're okay!" Ken answered smiling at his son.

Mark rubbed his head where he was hit and gave Jerry a death stare. He smirked back at Mark and felt like he needed to add a little fuel to the fire as they all turned to leave.

"Hey Mark, I'm a little curious. What did you come back here for?" Jerry asked already knowing the answer and knew the trouble it would compound onto his brother.

Mr. Davis stopped and waited for an answer from his older son.

"I was, uh." Mark stumbled through his answer and Jerry hit him with the final blow.

"What's that red thing sticking out of your back pack?"

Mark cringed at the inquiry and realized he forgot that the backpack with the dress and wig was still on his back.

Mr. Davis noticed it now as the light from the fire shimmered off the red sequins sewn into the dress.

"What the?"

Mr. Davis pulled the red dress from the bag and the blonde wig tumbled out with it onto the ground. He stared at it for a second, looked at Mark and then over to Ken.

"I'm not sure what's going on here and I'm not sure if I want to know, but when we get home, you will explain yourself, young man." Mr. Davis demanded with a stern jaw. "Ken, I apologize for my son's behavior and for bothering you on this Saturday evening."

Ken looked at the wig laying on the ground and shook his head laughing.

"I can't wait to hear this story."

He looked at his son Dirk and addressed him directly.

"I will see you bright and early in the morning son. Don't forget, we have church."

"Yes sir!" Dirk answered as he pushed a marshmallow onto his hanger and placed it over the fire. Jerry followed his lead and did the same while holding back an incredible urge to laugh out loud.

The four of them left the camp site and made their way back home through the pasture without much conversation. Mark gave Duke the occasional confused glance, wondering what the heck had just happened and worried about the consequences he would endure back at home.

CHAPTER 11

As soon as the boys felt like they were out of earshot, they erupted into uncontrollable laughter and fell to the ground around the fire. Jerry sat up with tears in his eyes and spoke through the laughter.

"Did you see the look on Mark's face when he saw us here?

"Yes, it looked like his eyes were gonna pop out of his head." Dirk agreed dusting the dirt from his pants.

The laughter eventually subsided and the seriousness of what they had witnessed earlier in the night started to creep in. Jerry sat on the stump again while Dirk found a spot on

82

the fallen tree opposite the fire. They both loaded another marshmallow onto their hangers and the brief stint of silence was interrupted by Dirk.

"Why do you think she showed us that?"

"I don't know, but she sure is anxious to show us more."

"Are you seriously thinking of going back there?" Dirk asked twisting the hanger over the fire.

"Aren't you curious?" Jerry asked back.

"Yes. Very curious, but I'm only going back if you're going."

"Let's go tomorrow after church." Jerry offered.

"All the parents will be watching football so it will be easier to sneak away."

"Okay." Dirk agreed and laid back across the old tree to look at the stars. Dirk stared up at the sky and listened to the crickets playing their songs while looking for the first sighting of a shooting star. Jerry finished his last marshmallow and joined him on the other end of the tree. It didn't take long before the conversation turned back to Penny.

"What else do you think she was trying to show us Jerry?"

"I don't know, but I'm sure we'll find out tomorrow."

"Do you think she's watching us right now?" Dirk asked.

"If she is, I don't wanna know." Jerry answered and was quick to change the subject. "You wanna go catch some lightening bugs?"

Dirk sat up realizing Jerry didn't want to discuss Penny anymore and jumped down from the tree.

"Sure, let's go."

The two of them traced the trail through the woods and stepped out from the tall blood weed bushes into the pasture. Lightening bugs filled the night sky and the boys spent hours running around snatching them from the air. They would cup their hands together and peek in to watch the bugs light up and took comfort in forgetting about Penny for a while.

@@@@@

Other than the occasional roar of football fans cheering their teams from their living rooms, the neighborhood streets were quiet. Jim and Ken talked about work and college football as the road changed from gravel to pavement when they entered the cul-de-sac. Jim walked up his driveway with Mark and Duke following close behind after apologizing multiple times and saying goodnight to his good friend and neighbor Ken. Jim told Mark to say goodnight to Duke as well and they watched him gladly speed away on his bicycle. He was relieved not having to witness the wrath of Mr. Davis and hoped there would be no phone call to his parents. Mark attempted to step onto the front porch, but was halted by his Dad.

"Just a minute son?" Jim grabbed him by the arm. "What was going on out there?"

"We were just messing around trying to scare them, but when we got out there, we couldn't find them." Mark explained.

"So why the red dress and wig?" Jim was curious.

Mark lowered his head and knew his Dad would not like the answer.

"Remember the girl that went missing back there? I was gonna dress up like the ghost of Penny Myers and scare the pants off them."

Jim sighed deeply and with crossed arms chose his words carefully.

"Do you think it's wise to make fun of such a tragedy?" Jim explained. "Her parents lost their little girl and still have no answers to what happened to her. They have to live with that every day and I can't imagine what they are still going through. One day when you have kids, you will understand."

"Yes sir!" Mark stared at his shoes as guilt built up inside of him and he began to cry.

"I guess we won't have to discuss this again, right?" Jim Davis was stern, but shared a little pain with his son.

"No sir." Mark answered through tears and went inside to his room.

Jim sat on the front porch looking out at the darkened street with sporadic spots of light and the thought of Penny Myers invaded his mind. Although she didn't live in the neighborhood, her disappearance made an impact on the community and every parent mourned with the Myers family. The picture that was printed of Penny and stapled to every telephone pole was an image that was burned into his mind. Jim remembered helping in the search for weeks and couldn't believe not one shred of evidence was ever found. It didn't make sense, he thought and wondered how no one had seen or heard anything. There were workers across the canal welding and painting and not one of them saw a thing.

The only reports that did surface were kids seen swimming in the cove, but none matching the description of Penny. Chances were most of those kids were his and he knew they swam there without permission from time to time. How could he scold them for doing the same thing he grew up doing? The memories of those times made him think of his own kids and brought tears to his eyes. Brenda stood inside at the screen door looking out at her husband and wanted to ask what was up, but realized now probably wasn't the right time. Jim sat there reflecting for a while, prayed for the Myers family once again and retired to the living room with his wife.

@@@@@

When Penny opened her eyes, she felt the warmth of a bright light above her. Her eyes were trying to focus on something, anything that was familiar. She heard music in the distance, but couldn't place the song or band and she was pretty good at that. Where was she? She was laying on something soft and tried to get up, but couldn't move her limbs and her body felt heavy. She tried to remember where she was last. What was she doing before this? Her mind scrambled for an answer. *The platform*, she thought. She remembered now. She was on top of the platform and saw Michael on the shore. She lost her balance and fell into the water. Then she was inside the platform bleeding, gasping for air and from inside the space she remembers seeing Michael and someone else on the bank. Everything went dark again and she felt cold and alone.

Now she was in this comfortable, warm place. Where was she? She tried again to move her hand, but it wouldn't budge. Suddenly a flushed feeling came over her and she floated up and off the soft spot. She was moving now, flying somewhere and the warm lights were fading. The heaviness in her arms and legs was fading too and she could move her hands now. She put her right hand in front of her face and stared at it. Her fingers were blurred, seemed longer than usual and she tried hard to focus on them. The area around her became dark and the movement stopped. She tried straining her eyes to see something, anything. Then silence, the music was gone.

Just before the feeling of panic overcame her, she started to move again and noticed a small light in the distance that was getting closer. The light expanded into a 360-degree aerial view of the farm and she was moved in closer. Penny had no control and she didn't like this feeling. She stopped moving just above the trees and watched from above as her parents and a large group of people stood beneath her, holding each other as they wept.

She tried to call them, but there was no sound. She opened her mouth wider and screamed as loud as she could at them, but there was still no sound. Getting more frustrated, she started flailing her arms to attempt to get closer, but it was no use. She sat suspended in the air with no control of anything and felt helpless. Her Dad looked up at the sky with his eyes filled with tears and she felt the pain he was enduring. In an instant, everything went dark again while Penny closed her eyes and held onto the vision of her Dad's face.

CHAPTER 12

Smoke rose slowly from what was left of the boy's smoldering fire and whispered away up into the trees above the campsite. The cool morning air chilled the inside of the tent while both boys were completely zipped up into their sleeping bags and looked like two overweight caterpillars. Dirk was the first to move and as he took a deep breath of the crisp air, the urge suddenly hit him. He crawled out of his bag, unzipped the tent and stood barefoot in the dirt next to the fire. He took aim and relieved himself while helping to extinguish the fire. The smoke dampened a bit and flowed low past Dirk and into the half-opened tent door. Within seconds he heard movement inside and then the words came.

"Dude, that's gross! Jerry complained and was quick to exit the urine scented smoke-filled tent.

"Early bird gets first dibs!" Dirk said laughing. "You're just mad because I got you first."

"Whatever." Jerry quipped and stood next to him joining in on the extinguishment.

"What time is it?" Jerry asked looking up at the trees trying to gauge it from the morning sunlight.

Dirk looked at the Timex on his wrist and squinted his burning eyes.

"It's 8:00."

"We have to get going. I cannot be late for church and I'm sure Dad isn't in the best of moods this morning."

"Yeah, mine either." Jerry agreed.

The boys threw a few buckets of water on the fire just to be sure and loaded up all the gear in their back packs. They stood on the bank and watched a tug boat pass by and although both of them thought of Penny, neither spoke of her. They would attend church as normal and when the parents were deep into the football game, they would return as promised and hopefully have a few more answers to the mystery of Penny Myers.

@@@@@

Just after lunch, Dirk sat on the front porch swing waiting for Jerry after asking for him through the front screen door. Mark had answered the door when Dirk knocked and didn't appear to be very happy to see him. He was still feeling the brunt of whatever prank Dirk and his brother had pulled on him by hiding from him and Duke.

Dirk swung back and forth and his attention was redirected behind him as the sound of a crow beckoned to be heard. It sat on the cyclone fence with a wing extended picking its feathers and cawing with a harsh tone. Dirk sat staring at it as it seemed to look right back at him. It continued to caw and suddenly took flight when the screen door flew open. It slammed against the wall and made a loud clacking noise as Jerry stormed out of the house. He stopped at the end of the porch near the steps with his hands on his hips and Dirk could tell something was wrong, but sat there quietly.

"I can't go!" Jerry said with clinched fists.

"Why? Dirk moved towards him.

"I have to cut the grass and it's going to take all afternoon."

"Why today?"

"My parents are going to watch the game at my uncle's house and we were supposed to cut it yesterday. It doesn't matter, I can't go!" Jerry explained and sat on the steps with his arms crossed.

"It's okay, we can try to go tomorrow after school?" Dirk offered.

"No Dirk, you have to go today. We promised and she'll be waiting on us." Jerry tensed up.

"Oh, I don't know man. Not sure I want to go in alone." Dirk whispered showing concern.

"You have to. Trust me, you'll be fine. Besides, it'll give you two a little time alone." Jerry laughed.

Dirk joined his friend on the steps and finally agreed to go, but just to tell Penny that they would both return on Monday. He wasn't going to go in the stump and swore he would be back later to help with the grass. He left Jerry with his chores and started the long walk down the fence to the pasture. The black crow that left the fence abruptly flew high above him unnoticed and followed Dirk as he walked. It circled in the sky like a buzzard over a dead animal and drew in closer as Dirk made it to the spot.

Dirk stopped at the fence and surveyed the area to make sure he wasn't followed. When he knew it was clear, he crossed through and headed down the dirt road towards the bayou. The large crow descended lower, landed on a rotten branch of a scrub oak above the fence and watched Dirk pass through. Its eyes glowed green sparkling in the midday sun while it picked at its feathers again. The crow waited for Dirk to clear the fence, then flew through the middle wires and just like Dirk, vanished on the other side.

@@@@@

"So where were you guys?" Mark asked Jerry as he poured gas into the tank of the lawnmower.

"We were right where you and Dad found us!" Jerry explained again.

"No, you weren't there the first time we came out there. Duke and I walked through the campsite and there was nothing there. No gear, no fire and no spoiled brat!" Mark finished pouring the gas and slammed the cap back on the tank.

"We were there!" Jerry insisted and grabbed the cane knife and left the shed. He knew the interrogation would continue outside. Mark pushed the mower out of the shed and continued.

"I'm not sure where you were, but I'm gonna find out." Mark threatened as he pulled the cord to crank the mower. It started after the third try and he began the long tedious task of cutting two acres of grass with a push mower. He and Jerry would swap out here and there with trimming the yard by hand with the cane knife, but even still it was their least favorite thing to do on a Sunday. They both welcomed the colder weather and the shunting of the grass growth and were jealous of their sisters who only did inside work.

Jerry crawled around the edge of the house and fence swinging the knife and bagging the clippings as he moved. He went through the motions and continued his chores, but his mind was elsewhere. He thought of Dirk and Penny and battled with the idea of possibly missing whatever it was she wanted to show them. He was still trying to wrap his mind around the place on the other side and had some concern about Dirk being alone back there. He was the one who always pushed the envelope when they tried new things. When he wanted to ride his bike through the ditch, Dirk wanted to fill it with burning gasoline, build a wooden ramp and jump over it. Two broken bones and three sets of stitches could be attributed to the challenges he accepted from Dirk through the years. He would worry about his friend today with the combination of the power on the other side and the vivid imagination of Dirk Matherne.

@@@@@

The vision of her Dad sobbing was burned into Penny's mind and she beckoned to understand from the deepest part of her soul. She was alone and felt suspended in the air like a puppet being controlled by its master. She had no control and though she hated that feeling, something else made her feel at peace. The darkness was interrupted by a light in the distance and Penny felt a presence there. There was no form or shape, but definitely a presence. Penny had questions, but no words were spoken, only thoughts and feelings were exchanged.

Where am I?

You're right where you need to be for now, Penny. You're safe and will no longer feel pain. I will be with you through the transition.

Who are you?

I'm a friend and someone you can trust, Penny. I will bring you somewhere and help you to understand.

Penny closed her eyes and she felt her body being moved again. In the distance, she could make out a silhouette of a tree line and whatever force that was controlling her, set her down softly amongst a trove of cypress trees and released her. She could see everything now and her bare feet rested gently on a soft cover of grass. Through the cover of trees, multiple beams of sunlight made their way to the surface of the swamp. The jet-black water sparkled like diamonds in places where the sunlight hit and long strands of moss from the tree branches seemed to be reaching down for a drink. She felt a little more at ease being back on the ground and the thought of being alone in the marsh seemed different now. A good kind of different, but she was still full of questions.

She stood on the edge of a swamp near a large cypress stump that towered ten feet above her head and she tried to communicate again.

Are you still here with me?

Yes, I'll always be here with you.

Why am I here?

You are here to help them understand what happened and I'm here to help you. I'm going to give you certain powers, Penny and some time to figure it out. Use your imagination, you are so good at that.

Penny moved over to the stump, pulled the moss back on a flattened part of it, closed her eyes and imagined a small door with a staircase that descended below the ground. When she opened her eyes, it was there. She stepped carefully down the stairs and let her imagination run wild. She felt like she had more control now and spent hours designing a new world for herself. Penny still didn't understand it and truly felt it was all a dream. She may as well have fun with it until she woke up, she told herself.

CHAPTER 13

The large oak trees that surrounded the parking lot drew shade over most of the spots and Jerry and Dirk had rolled the windows down to enjoy the breeze. "Do you regret meeting her?" Jerry asked while keeping an eye on the man at the front door of the attorney's office.

"I don't regret anything. What happened, happened for a reason. Look, Jerry, you know I'm not a very religious person, but I do feel that God had a hand in this and for whatever reason, this is how it's supposed to be." Dirk continued. "It's not my job or nature to question God. He put Penny in our lives for a reason. Maybe it was to show us that the decisions we were making, weren't the right ones. Do you know how many people would jump at the chance to do what we did?"

"Yes, everyone I know would and some that I don't!"

Before he could finish, another vehicle pulled into the lot and captured their attention.

"That's gotta be Webb." Jerry said.

The driver of the black, 2017 Maserati Ghibli eased into the lot and parked three spaces over from the SUV. The large man in the suit adjusted his stance and was also captured by the lure of such an incredible car. It was spotless and as it moved slowly through the lot, the reflection of the large oak trees above it glimmered across the paint. It had obviously been detailed within the hour. The driver stepped from the vehicle, set the alarm with his key fob and entered the office in a purposeful manner.

"That was him!" Dirk said.

"Let's go, it's time!" Jerry said looking at his watch.

"Yep, let's get this over with." Dirk added and reached for the door handle.

Dirk and Jerry eased across the parking lot and approached the front door of the office. Surprisingly, the man that had been standing guard at the door greeted them, smiled and opened the door. Upon entering the office, they gave each other a puzzled look and was greeted again by the receptionist.

"Can I help you gentlemen?" A short brunette asked from behind the desk.

"We're here for a 1:00 appointment with Mr. Webb." Dirk spoke up.

"Ah yes, you must be Mr. Davis and Mr. Matherne? They are all here waiting for you, right this way." The receptionist led the two of them to a large office in the rear of the building and opened the door. Dirk was the first to enter and when he saw the lady from the SUV sitting at the table, something was very familiar about her.

"You okay buddy, you look kind of pale." Jerry asked.

Dirk stared across the table at the young lady and couldn't figure out where he knew her from.

"Can I get you guys anything else besides water?" Mr. Webb offered from the other side of the table.

"No, I'm fine." Dirk answered trying not to be too obvious about staring. The woman under the hat and behind the glasses adjusted in her seat with a gesture of uneasiness. Dirk took a sip of water from a glass directly in front of him. His hand shook as he lowered it to the stone coaster and he swallowed hard. His eyes darted around the room and then stopped on the woman in the hat again.

How do I know her? He thought.

@@@@@

The envelope marked confidential that Dirk received a month prior to the meeting came with the last delivery of the evening from the local UPS driver. He left it at the door and rang the bell twice as he usually did to alert the occupant that mail had arrived. The smaller standard white envelope inside of the big yellow envelope had the business name of Thibodeaux & Webb, Attorneys at Law embossed in the upper left corner. Dirk A. Matherne was typed across the middle of it and Dirk was a little impressed with the professionalism of its appearance. He had received many letters from law offices before, asking for possible law suits against certain medical devices or illegal cell phone charges, but never one that looked so perfect. Those types were usually torn in half and discarded before they made it inside. This one caught his attention and he stopped just short of the kitchen door to open it.

After carefully ripping the edge and gaining access to the folded letter inside, his eyes quickly darted around the page looking for anything familiar. After getting nowhere with that process, he decided to settle down and read it like a normal person.

Mr. Matherne, your presence is requested at the above addressed location on June 30th promptly at 1:00 P.M. to hear the last will and testament of a person who will be disclosed at that time. You and one other person that is named in this letter are the only ones that are invited to this meeting. Your discreetness in this matter is appreciated and sharing this information with anyone not involved could affect the outcome of the dispersal of monies and/or property. We hope you will attend this proceeding on the date and time mentioned above and look forward to working with you in the near future.

Sincerely, Louis Webb

Thibodeaux & Webb LLP

Houma, La.

"What the heck is this?" Dirk mumbled, shaking his head. "Boy, these guys are getting good. I fell for it again!" Dirk laughed and tossed the letter and envelopes into the trash can near the door. He pressed the button on the wall and the garage door made its noisy way down to the floor as he entered the kitchen. Dirk walked over to the fridge and rifled through it looking for anything that looked even remotely edible. He found some leftover jambalaya he had cooked a few days earlier and reached for a plate from the cabinet next to the sink. The ring tone of Jimmy Buffet came from his cell phone on the counter as he scooped food onto the plate. He stopped what he was doing and grabbed the phone when he recognized the area code.

"Hello?"

"Hey buddy!" A familiar voice spoke on the other end and Dirk immediately knew who it was.

"Hey man, what's up? It's been a while." Dirk said.

"Oh, you know just down here living the dream." Jerry answered. How are things over in sunny Florida?" He continued with small talk.

"Doing well, man. Thanks for asking. I've been following you on social media. It looks like you are doing very well yourself." Dirk kept the pace.

After a short pause, Jerry broke the silence.

"Hey buddy, this may sound crazy, but did you get a letter from an attorney's office from here in Houma?"

The hair on the back of Dirk's neck stood at attention and the phone went silent for a few seconds.

"As a matter of fact, I just got one in the mail today." Dirk eased out of the kitchen door to the garbage can, pulled it from the trash and read the heading again.

"It was from a law firm called Thibodeaux and Webb. Why?"

"Because I got the same letter." Jerry

answered.

Dirk scanned the bottom of the page in notes and noticed Jerry's name in bold print as a second party.

"Yes, I see your name now, I don't know how I missed it. I thought it was just another piece of junk mail. I get them all the time, ya know." Dirk explained.

"I know, so do I!" Jerry agreed. "So, do you think this is legit?"

"I'm not sure, but can't you call or go by there and find out?" Dirk asked.

"I'm sure I can. What do you think this is about?"

"Probably some girl you slept with back in college and she is coming to collect child support." Dirk joked.

"Very funny! Well, not that funny to be honest. I may have a few possibilities out there." Jerry responded.

"I have no idea what it's about, but I gotta tell ya, I'm curious to find out. Let me know what you come up with and if it sounds like it's the real deal, I'll make a trip down there." Dirk explained.

"Okay buddy. I'll call you tomorrow."

Dirk hung up the phone, set the microwave for 2 minutes and looked forward to the leftovers.

CHAPTER 14

Dirk continued down the dirt path still amazed by the surroundings and decided to play around.

"Butterfly" Dirk said out loud as he carefully crossed the cattle guard.

Within seconds a blue and yellow butterfly with red spots flew around his head and landed on his shoulder.

"Walking stick" he said and a hand carved stick appeared in his hand. As he used it to walk, Dirk smiled, left the dirt road and continued his way through the pasture. His mind wandered and he thought of many things, but decided to be careful and keep it simple for now. He strolled through the tall grass as it swayed in the breeze and it looked like an ocean of green with rising and falling waves. The path that he and Jerry had made was still flattened and the cool temperature of the grass felt good on his bare feet. Large puffy white clouds rimmed with multiple colors passed by overhead and would block the sunlight in some places on the ground. Dirk made a game of it and started to run trying to stay in the shady places of the shadows. The butterfly followed close behind and seemed to be enjoying the game as well. Before long, he made it to the blood weed, pushed through to the other side and entered the woods. The stick he carried disappeared from his hand and the butterfly was nowhere to be found. Just like before it all went away in the woods.

Dirk approached the marsh with a little caution and slowed when he rounded the corner and saw the stump. Perched gracefully on top of the stomp was a crow and it seemed to welcome Dirk, this time with a warm softened caw. Its eyes glowed green in the shadowed woods and Dirk's jaw dropped.

"Penny?" He whispered, tilting his head.

The crow flapped its wings and rose from the stump and floated above the path in front of him. A bright light formed on its chest and began to grow outward in all directions. The light blinded Dirk so he turned his head and stepped back and braced himself against a tree. When it began to fade Dirk watched from behind his closed hand as her body came into focus. She wore a beautiful white dress trimmed with flowers and her long curly blonde hair hung past her shoulders. She was beautiful, he thought.

"I knew you'd come back, Dirk." Penny spoke softly.

"It was you on the fence, wasn't it? How?" Dirk asked still amazed at the transformation he just witnessed.

"Yes, it was me. I've been watching you Dirk."

"Why?" Dirk seemed confused.

"I needed to be sure you're the right one." Penny moved closer and reached for his hand. Her green eyes piercing through him again.

"Right one for what?" Dirk asked.

"That's what I want to show you." She said and turned towards the stump.

"No, wait Penny. Dirk pulled back a little. I told Jerry I would only come to let you know that he couldn't come and we would both be here tomorrow." Dirk explained.

"I know that Dirk. I was there and saw what happened. It's perfect now, because you need to see this alone. Please, Dirk?" Penny begged.

"Why?" Dirk asked, more confused now.

"I need to show you this alone. I used Jerry just to get you back here, but he's not the one I need." Penny confessed. "You are Dirk. You're the only one that will understand and follow through. You will understand when you see it, and tomorrow may be too late." Penny pushed again.

Dirk's mind was reeling and he was getting very nervous, but he felt her warmth and for some reason trusted her. He felt a deep need to help her and she made him feel like he was the only one that could. He battled with the promise he made with Jerry, but also knew he would understand. Dirk followed Penny into the stump and just as before stood in the room with the watery window and his heart was about to beat out of his chest.

@@@@@

Jerry rubbed his sore hands and picked at a blister that had formed on his hand. He hated trimming the grass with the cane knife and wondered when someone would invent a better tool. His right arm ached from swinging the knife back and forth so he took a quick break for some water. As he drank from the water hose he noticed Mark was about finished with his part of using the mower and welcomed a trading of chores. Mark was about 30 feet from finishing up when the mower started to sputter until it finally shut off. He left it where it was and walked towards Jerry and the running water hose.

"Give me that hose, ya Brat." Mark took the hose from Jerry and drank from it like a crazed animal.

"I wasn't finished drinking yet!" Jerry said as he stepped back.

"You can have it when I'm done." Mark squawked and continued to drink.

"It's almost my turn on the mower." Jerry smiled.

"Good, you may wanna put some gas in it though!" Mark said laughing.

"You ran it out, you fill it up." Jerry said angered.

"It's your turn," Mark said and walked towards the fence where Jerry left the knife and bag.

"Jerk." Jerry said under his breath when Mark was far enough away not to hear.

He took another sip, turned off the hose and went to the shed for the gas can. Jerry could hold his own in a fight, but was always careful not to push his siblings too far. Mark was the only brother still at home and was five years older and quite bigger than Jerry. He played football when he was younger, but had more success in baseball as he got older. Mark made the Varsity team when he was a freshman, but lost interest and found himself in trouble over the last two years. He was suspended from the team for fighting with his team mates and finally kicked off for punching an umpire after a bad call at home plate. From that point, his grades dropped and there was talk of sending him to a military school in Mississippi. When Jim Davis finally put his foot down and started spending a little more time at home, Mark straightened up and salvaged what was left of his junior year. He was now a senior, and had a renewed sense of purpose and was looking forward to moving away to attend college somewhere out of state. That was his plan, anyway.

Jerry returned with the gas can and filled the empty tank on the mower. It was always hard to see when it was full and as usual he stopped pouring when it bubbled out over the rim. He placed the can to the side and after about six cranks, the mower sputtered some and then fired up. He picked up where Mark left off and tediously pushed the mower back and forth to finish his portion of the two acres.

He thought of Dirk and Penny again and was hoping to see his buddy walk through the back gate any minute with the latest news, but that wasn't the case. They finished the grass when it was just about dark and carried the bags of clippings to the back fence where it would be burned when it dried out. Jerry took a quick bath and then sat on the front swing looking at the latest issue of MAD magazine that he cleverly borrowed from his brother. He liked the *Spy vs. Spy* cartoon the best and was about to finish it when he heard the phone ring. Mark yelled at Jerry from somewhere inside the house and told him to grab the phone. Jerry dropped the magazine on the swing and made it to the wall by the 4th ring.

"Hello?" He asked out of breath.

"Hey, Jerry can you tell Dirk to come on home, it's time for his supper?"

Jerry paused to answer and chose his words carefully trying to avoid getting him in trouble.

"Yes ma'am, I will tell him as soon as he gets back. He said he was going to look for his flashlight and thought he may have dropped it on the way back from the woods this morning."

"Oh dear! Okay, will you tell him when he returns please?" Mrs. Matherne asked with slight concern.

"I sure will ma'am." Jerry assured.

He hung up the phone and returned to the swing and started to worry that things didn't go as planned with Penny. He should have been back by now, he thought.

CHAPTER 15

Jack Murphy shoved through the tight, cluttered spaces of his dark home carrying a flashlight in one hand and a bullwhip in the other. He wore a dirty white T-shirt, oversized, black warm up pants and a food stained robe with no belt. His cowboy hat was old, torn on one side and sat way too low on his head, covering his greasy thinning hair. His slippers were soiled with pet urine and feces that was riddled throughout the old worn out carpet in the once immaculate home. The house was cluttered and stacked from floor to ceiling with old books and garbage leaving only a small trail from room to room. There were two working light bulbs in the entire house and the walls, doors and windows showed multiple signs of disrepair.

The stress of losing their son and the death of their niece on the property was too much to take for Mrs. Murphy. She left Jack and their home one year after the accident and moved to her sister's place in Texas. She couldn't take the pressure of seeing her son in a locked facility and the man she married and bore a child with was long gone.

Jack Murphy was lost somewhere inside of himself and in most of the neighbor's opinion, had gone off the deep end. The man that was once a strong, happy and successful farm owner was now an old, broken down, senile recluse.

The farm stayed in business for a while, but quickly started to deteriorate when Jack became depressed and in fits of rage would fire the staff for minimal things. The clientele from the horse business fell off as well when the news spread about Joe, the riding trainer, getting fired. Sadly, some of the horses died from neglect, but most of them were taken away to a rehab ranch nearby.

Also, Jack would take in any stray dog that came around for food and they ran in and out of the house freely. Any family left, that used to visit, quit coming because of the shape and smell of the home. When social services were finally called, Jack would put on his best show and do just enough legally to be able to stay. He told everyone that tried to get him help or out of the home that he would have to be dead to leave.

Jack squeezed through the tiny space in the dining room on the way to the kitchen, set his bullwhip on the counter and opened the fridge. Food in various stages of molding sat on the shelves of the fridge as Jack moved things around to look for something still edible. He slipped his flashlight into the pocket of his robe and leaned in close. Jack pulled out an opened can of potted meat and grabbed a semi clean spoon that rested in filth at the bottom of the sink. A cockroach scurried under a stack of dirty dishes for protection and Jack ignored it. He raised the can to his nose and sniffed it like a dog would do to a new brand of dog food in his bowl. Approving of the scent, he took bites from the can and made his way back to his bedroom where he spent most of his time.

Jack pulled his flashlight out of his pocket to light up the pathway and stopped in the hallway when something caught his attention. It seemed to be moving near the bathroom at the other end of the hall. When he moved the light in that direction, he gasped for air and dropped his supper and spoon on the floor.

The image of Penny Myers floated just above the floor of the hallway. Her body was dripping with water and wearing only panties and a bra she looked angelic. Her hair hung heavy, wet, straight down with no curls and was stained with bright red blood. The light accentuated the color of the blood and it flowed down her shoulders, onto her arms and dripped from her fingers to the floor.

The sight of her frightened Jack and he fell back against the door of his bedroom, grabbed his chest and looked away. Breathing heavily and facing the den now, Jack gathered himself after a minute and slowly raised the light back in the direction of the bathroom. He was relieved that she was gone. Several times he turned the light on and off making sure of it. This was the first time he had seen her or at least thought he had seen her since the accident. Was his mind playing tricks on him, he thought?

Jack picked up the only supper he had left and rubbed the spoon against his robe as if to clean it. The rocking chair that sat in a small corner of his bedroom under a dull lamp waited for him like an old friend. The seat made of wicker with oak trim was shredded in places, but was still able to hold his weight. Jack sat rocking back and forth thinking of better times, attempting to rid his mind of what he thought he saw. He finished what was left in the half empty can while one of the only two light bulbs left in the house, flickered above his head and then burnt out.

@@@@@

Michael heard Mark's voice, turned abruptly still covering his eyes with both hands and recognized him through his fingers. He dropped his hands and pointed to the water and screamed.

"Penny!"

Mark ran down from the hill where he was concealed in the trees and looked at him confused as most people did when he went off into one of his fits of rage. Michael struggled with communication when he was calm, but when he was excited, it was even worse.

"Penny, who's Penny, Michael?" Mark asked looking at the water for the girl he had also seen fall.

"Penny's hurt!" Michael screamed and hit himself again.

"Calm down, Michael. Who is she?" Mark asked again, getting frustrated. He walked around the tree to the edge of the bank and looked for any movement or bubbles in the water. He saw nothing and turned to Michael again who had sat on the tree sobbing.

"Is that Penny in the water, Michael?" Mark grilled him.

Michael pointed to the water and then covered his face again. Mark walked over to him and noticed Penny's clothes on the ground near Michael's feet.

Mark had known Michael as long as he could remember and always felt sorry for him. When kids from the neighborhood would tease him, Mark would take the higher road and protect him. It wasn't always easy and he would often get into trouble after fighting with a few of them.

They watched the barge pass and then the water returned to the cove in a rush of muddy looking soup. Mark took off his shoes and swam out to the platform where he too, had seen her fall. He descended underwater with his eyes open searching for any sign of her, but it was pointless. The visibility in this water was about two inches and he knew he would have to feel for her to find her. He returned to the surface and moved to shallower water to drag his feet on the muddy bottom in a desperate attempt to feel anything.

Michael continued to pace rubbing his face and head and was no help to Mark.

After thirty minutes of searching the cove, Mark collapsed in the shallow water near the bank and stared out at the Intracoastal. He was exhausted and his lungs burned from holding his breath. The small buzz that he was feeling from the beer was long gone. He wondered who the girl was because she did not look familiar. Maybe a cousin of Michael's, he thought.

Mark climbed up onto the bank and sat next to Michael. Fear filled Mark's body as his mind fought with the options of what to do. He could run home, he thought and call the police, but he knew by the time they would conduct a search, it would be too late. She was dead by now, he was convinced of that and any report of a girl being missing back there would put blame on him or Michael. If he left now and didn't say a word, Michael would be blamed for it and he wouldn't be able to communicate what happened. That was his way out, but could he live with that? The only evidence left was the girl's clothes and he could get rid of them somewhere.

Mark stood from the dead tree and made the decision to act. He had to get rid of the clothes, threaten Michael to keep quiet and hope that he would understand enough to do so. He gathered the clothes and walked towards the far end of the cove and stopped near a tree next to the water. He knelt on the ground and used his hands to dig a hole in the dirt. Mark pulled a lighter from his pocket and lit the clothes on fire. He dropped them in the hole and within minutes the clothes were burnt and Mark began covering them up with dirt and leaves. He found a few broken branches nearby and covered the freshly removed dirt. Michael stayed sitting on the tree rubbing his face as Mark finished what he was doing and went back to check on Michael.

"Are you okay, Michael?" Mark asked as he cleaned his hands in the bayou. There was no response.

"We need to go now." Mark put his hand on his shoulder and squeezed it.

Michael stood and walked toward the trail and made no mention of Penny on the way home. He sang the Gilligan's Island theme song repeatedly as they crossed the pasture and came to the fence behind the Murphy's. Mark tried to ignore the annoying song and helped Michael through the fence into his yard. Mark said goodbye, reminded Michael of their secret and prayed that he would understand to keep quiet.

CHAPTER 16

At 9:00 PM the Davis' phone on the wall rang multiple times and Jerry sat on the swing purposely not answering it. Mark was watching the end of a football game and finally grew tired of hearing it so he picked it up. Jerry moved over to the screen door so he could at least hear one side of the conversation. He was pretty sure it was Dirk's mother looking for him.

"No ma'am, I haven't seen him. Yes ma'am. Okay, we'll keep an eye out for him and let you know if he comes by here. Yes ma'am!"

Mark hung up the phone and returned to the couch to watch the game without another thought of Dirk. Jerry went back to the swing and really started worrying about his friend. If he didn't show up, how would he explain it? No one would believe him and if he showed them, it would ruin everything. He sat back on the swing kicked his feet forward and tried to think of something to say when the questions started.

Headlights appeared in the driveway and Jerry already knew the game was decidedly over and the Saints had lost. If his parents were home early, he knew it was too late for some miraculous comeback and his Dad couldn't bear to watch the end of another depressing loss. He slipped inside the house before they saw him and made his way to the tub for a quick bath. He could hear Mark and his Dad discussing the game in the living room and then the phone rang again. He quickly dried himself, threw on some clothes and stood near the door to try to hear the conversation. He heard some mumbling through the door, but couldn't tell who his mom was talking to. Suddenly, a knock at the door startled him.

"Jerry, any idea where Dirk is? His mom is starting to worry." His mom's voice beckoned from the other side of the door.

Jerry didn't want to lie, but he had no choice.

"No ma'am. Not since he left to go look for his flashlight." Jerry answered while drying himself off. He had told Jerry he wasn't staying and he especially didn't think Dirk would stay this late back there by himself. Mrs. Davis returned to the phone and asked if there was anything they could do to help.

"Absolutely, I'm sure the boys and Jim wouldn't mind going help look for him. They'll be waiting for Kenny in the driveway."

She hung up with Barbara, told Jim the news of Dirk being missing and as Jerry listened from behind the door, a sinking feeling enveloped him. The stern voice of his Dad called for him from the living room and Jerry slowly poked around the corner. Jim sat on the edge of his recliner with a flashlight in his hand.

"Any idea where Dirk is?" Jim Davis asked with his chin down, eyes glaring over his reader glasses.

"No Dad, he said he was going to look for his flashlight and that's the last time I saw him." Jerry explained with no added details.

"You and Mark put on some shoes, we are going with his Dad to help look for him." Jim stood from the chair, gave Brenda a reassuring kiss and told her not to worry and that everything would be fine. Brenda had a bad feeling this was not the case and felt horrible for her friends.

Jerry threw on some shoes, met them in the driveway and noticed Dirk's Dad had a grim look on his face. Kenny knew his son well enough to know that if he wasn't home by now, something was wrong.

They all made their way through the pasture calling his name on occasion and looking for any signs of Dirk. They crossed the fence and spent a few hours searching the woods, marsh and anywhere else they thought he may go. Jerry followed along and played the part of a distraught friend, but knew they wouldn't find him. Not on this side of the fence anyway. He would keep the secret as long as he could or at least until he found out if Dirk was safe.

When they returned home without him, Barbara was beside herself with grief and begged Kenny to call the police. He was already thinking of that, but knew nothing would be done tonight and Dirk would not even be considered missing until after 24 hours. The authorities in a bigger city like New Orleans may take action earlier than that, but in a small town like Bourg, you would be lucky to see an officer before then. It's wasn't because they lacked the interest or skills, but manpower was always an issue and most of the force were volunteers. Even with the enormity in the disappearance of Penny Myers, the most they could afford to have working on her case at one time were five officers. The Terrebonne Parish Sheriff's Office eventually passed the case on to the New Orleans Police Department after exhausting all their means of investigating and wasting a bunch of time.

Kenny decided to wait until morning to get them involved and hoped Dirk would turn up before then. He had no idea where Dirk could be and he also started to worry as the memory of Penny Myers crept in. He sat on the front porch holding his wife and prayed his son would not be the second kid to disappear in those woods.

@@@@@

Penny slid her hand across the window like she was erasing a chalkboard and within seconds the blurred watery substance came into focus. Dirk moved closer to the window and recognized the scene again. It was the cove and he saw Penny methodically climbing the platform all the way to the top. She stood there for a second and then he saw her trying to cover her half naked body again just like before. He heard a boy's voice screaming something and then she lost her balance and fell backwards. On the way down, she hit her head on a plank that jutted out and then she splashed into the water. Dirk watched in amazement now from under the water as Penny sunk motionless for a while and then she started to struggle. The current from the passing barge pulled at her and he saw her get sucked into the void of the platform. He noticed she hit her head when she surfaced underneath the platform and then became still again after she managed to pull herself up. Blood flowed profusely from the two large cuts on her head and she managed to call out for help, but only in a whisper. Dirk watched as the life left her body and her skin turned pale. Now he understood.

"It was an accident." Dirk said under his breath as he stared at the window. He watched Michael losing control, screaming her name and hitting himself. He then saw him return to the fallen tree and start to cry. Stepping closer to the window he saw someone else now and could hear a conversation. Dirk stood next to Penny and she grabbed his hand as she revealed who it was.

"What are you doing back here, Michael?" The familiar voice was amplified in the tiny room and echoed against the walls.

Dirk stood petrified and confused as he saw Mark jump into the water to look for Penny.

"Mark?" Dirk mumbled then his mouth awkwardly dropped open. He watched him panicking and thrashing around in the water desperately looking for her.

"Yes, Dirk. He was there watching me too." Penny said as she turned towards him.

Mark was hiding behind a tree watching her as she stripped down and swam in the cove. He was smoking a cigarette he had stolen from his mom and drinking one of the beers that he swiped from the fridge. The pony Miller Beers were just small enough to fit into his coat pockets and he often snuck out of the house on the weekends to find refuge and solitude at the cove.

"He knew what happened all this time and didn't say anything?" Dirk questioned.

"Yes, but he was scared, Dirk and didn't want to get blamed." Penny explained.

"I don't understand?" Dirk lowered his head.

"There's a lot you don't understand yet, but this is what you needed to see." Penny said and squeezed his hand tight.

"Why me? Why didn't you just show Jerry?" Dirk was still perplexed.

"Because Mark is his brother and I didn't know what he would do." Penny went on. "I had to make sure it would be someone who would let everyone know and I'm not sure how much time I have left."

"How am I supposed to explain this?" Dirk asked again. "They won't believe me. They'll put me away like Michael!"

"Show them where I am, Dirk." Convince Mark that he needs to tell the truth, that will help. Lead them to my body, they will investigate and see that it was an accident." Penny turned to face Dirk and pleaded with him. Her eyes were glowing again and she moved in even closer. "I know you can do it, Dirk!" Penny said, stroking his ego a little and continued. "My parents need closure and Michael needs to be released from that facility."

Dirk stared at the window and wasn't sure what to do. He tried feverishly to wrap his mind around the incident, but was having a hard time understanding. He needed to somehow convince Mark that he knew and it was time for him to tell the truth, but how? He would have to bring Mark here and show him. It was the only way.

CHAPTER 17

Jerry stared at the upper bunk from his bed while he listened to his older sister, Patricia hit the off switch of her alarm clock which meant it was 5:30 AM and a school day. A lava lamp sitting on the dresser illuminated a red glow throughout the room. He hadn't slept at all and wrestled with what he was going to tell his parents. He knew the questions were going to continue and sooner or later if Dirk didn't return, he would have to tell them the truth. The more he thought about it, the more it scared him. He had never spent the night on the other side, so maybe that had something to do with it. He had always left before nightfall, but often wondered what it would be like. If Dirk's Dad were to get the police involved, he would be interviewed for sure and then he would have to show them. To avoid this, he needed to get back to the other side alone and find Dirk before it all blew up. He rolled over in his bed exhausted, pulled the blankets over his head and started the show.

Mark's feet swung down from the upper bunk as he slid down off the edge like a zombie and then drug his feet all the way to the kitchen for breakfast. Jerry could smell something cooking from under the covers and knew his Mom was already starting her morning routine. She was always the first one up in the morning preparing breakfast and getting lunches packed. Jerry's stomach won the battle against exhaustion and he also made his way to the kitchen. He poured a cup of coffee milk and put way too much sugar in it as usual. He picked a spot at the table and sipped from the cup as his mom placed a plate of French toast in front of him. Although this was his favorite meal for breakfast the hunger he thought he had, turned to nausea and he quickly ran to the bathroom.

"What's wrong with him?" His Mom asked as Jerry bolted out of the kitchen.

"Must be love sick." Mark snickered.

"That's enough out of you, young man." She said as she threw a kitchen towel at Mark and followed Jerry to the bathroom. She peeked into the door and saw him kneeling in front of the toilet vomiting.

"Are you okay sweetie?" She asked from the door, but not expecting an answer. She grabbed a small towel, wet it and placed it on the edge of the sink before returning to the kitchen. Jerry finished after a few minutes, grabbed the towel from the sink and moaned while wiping his face. He wandered back into the kitchen, sat at the table and placed his face on the cool Formica table top.

"If you feel that bad, you can stay home today." His mom offered standing at the sink.

Jerry moaned again, slid his face off the table and made his way back to bed smothering himself under his thick flannel blanket. He did feel nauseated from not knowing what was going on with Dirk, but was also very good at acting sick. He had mastered the skill over the years and a quick finger down his throat would make him puke every time. He needed to be home alone today and his plan was coming together. There was a fine line of being just a little sick or sick enough to warrant a doctor's visit and he had his mother figured out. He kept his composure under the blanket while listening to Mark and his sisters preparing to leave. They scrambled around the house gathering homework assignments and books, grabbed their lunch bags and headed out into the dark towards the bus stop. Next, he heard his Dad having a short conversation with his Mom and then listened for the sound of the truck traveling down the shell drive towards the road. Four down and one to go he thought.

Brenda Davis sat on a bench in front her vanity and finished applying her makeup in preparation for her day. She had just started back as a substitute teacher at the local elementary school and was enjoying the feeling of worthiness again. Before the kids, she was a full time 2nd grade teacher and loved her job, but when the kids came she was needed a lot more at home and put her career aside for a while.

Jerry followed her activity through the house and just before she entered the room he slowly slid the heating pad down between the wall and the bed. His head beaded with sweat as she came into check on him one more time. She bent over the bed and placed the back of her hand on his forehead.

"You're burning up, honey,"

"I know, but I'll be okay" he answered in his most pathetic tone.

"Are you sure, baby? I can stay home."

"No Mom, I'll be fine." Jerry answered and gave her a quick smile.

"Okay, I'll call you at lunch. If you need anything before that, call the school." Brenda said and left the room.

Jerry turned towards the wall, waited to hear her car leave the drive and then he sprang out of bed and headed back to the kitchen for some French toast. He was proud of himself for pulling it off, but nervous about what he might find. He would eat his French toast, give his Mom time to get to school and get settled in before he attempted to leave. Jerry had to make sure she wouldn't return before he got back.

@@@@@

Paul Thompson rounded the corner of the dirt road on his Honda 3-wheeler and crossed the cattle guard on the South side of his property. At 7:00 A.M., the sun was just creeping up above the horizon which gave the pasture a slight orange glow. Dressed in his normal work clothes which consisted of thick brown corduroy pants and a long sleeve shirt, he looked like a man on a mission. His small frame was dwarfed by the large cowboy hat he wore and his boot shifted the gears as he picked up speed towards the barn. He scanned his property as he rode, like he usually did this time of morning looking for anything out of place. At times, some of his cattle would get stuck in the mud near the ditches and he would have to lasso them to pull them out. All the cattle were accounted for this morning after talking to one of his workers during the morning feed. Also, on occasion he would have to run off the local kids for playing on the fences or in the barn. Not to be mean, but for the fear of an accident or another lawsuit, he felt it necessary. He was part of the suit when the Myers lost their daughter on his property, but because he had the proper fencing and the right amount of no trespass signs, he was removed from any liability.

The milk crate which was temporarily attached to the handle bars was packed with fence repair items and two hammers protruded out from the top. Paul pulled up close to the fence on the edge of his property and stepped off the 3 - wheeler into the dirt. Grabbing a hammer and some tack nails, he made his way over to the fence to repair some loose barbed wire. The wire was tacked from the other side so Paul placed the hammer and jar of tacks through the fence and then stooped low through the wires onto the Murphy's property. He moved down the fence from post to post adding tacks where it was needed to tighten the wires. All of the posts were old and weathered and most of the tacks had rusted and came loose.

When he came to the next section, he noticed a newer post and the tacks were shiny like they had just been replaced. He studied the post and knew he hadn't replaced any sections, but obviously someone had changed this section. The next post down the line was also new. Paul hung his hammer from the top wire, removed his hat and scratched his head while he analyzed the fence. Even the wire looked different, he thought. He pulled a handkerchief from the back pocket of his pants, wiped the sweat that had formed on his brow and thought it was a good time to retrieve his cold-water bottle from the 3-wheeler. With one hand, he attempted to push the wire down to pass through, but as soon as he touched it, he felt a tremendous shock go through his body and everything went dark.

When Paul woke up ten minutes later, his head was pounding and his entire body was tingling. He was on his back in the dirt looking up at the clear blue sky, moaning while rubbing his head. He made a fist, then straightened his fingers and then made a fist again. His arms and legs felt weak and strange.

"What the hell was that?" He mumbled.

He sat up and tried to gather himself rubbing his head again with everything around him still a little fuzzy. He remembered having this feeling before when a few years earlier, he accidentally touched an electric fence, but he knew this fence wasn't energized.

Paul staggered to his feet and carefully retrieved his hat from the post. When he reached for his hammer, he noticed something very strange. The post was different now. The section of fence that appeared to be new before was now weathered and just like the others, had rusted tacks protruding in places. He looked both ways down the fence thinking he was maybe wrong, but now the fence and all the posts were the same. Again, he didn't understand. He cautiously touched the wire again, this time with the back of his hand and there was no shock. Shaking his head, Paul gathered up the jar of tacks and slid through the wires making his way back to the 3 - wheeler. He didn't feel well and thought it would be best to head back to his house and rest up a bit. He would return later in the afternoon to finish up with the fence, he thought.

Paul loaded up the supplies into the crate and slowly climbed back onto the seat. His fingers and toes were still tingling, but he did his best with the thumb throttle and gears to maneuver the 3 - wheeler back onto the road. As he looked over at the fence when he passed by, he noticed a large crow perched on one of the fence post and thought nothing of it. The crow pecked at the wooden post and then took flight to a higher location for a better view.

@@@@@

Finishing his breakfast, Jerry grabbed his backpack, looked at the clock to make sure it was past 9:00 A.M. and headed for the fence. He made it through the pasture in record time and the morning dew from the uncut grass soaked his tennis shoes. He approached the fence with caution and did his normal inspection to make sure he was alone. In the distance, he could hear the motor of Mr. Thompson's 3-wheeler so he paused for a second. He ducked behind some bushes and realized the sound was moving away from him so he continued to the fence. He dropped his backpack near the barbed wire and slipped through the fence. Reaching back through the fence to grab his backpack, he stopped when a second of confusion overcame him. He realized in his hurried attempt to get to Dirk, he crossed through the wrong section. Jerry laughed at himself and crossed back through to correct the mistake. As soon as he did, he realized it wasn't a mistake. He observed the fence posts with an opened jaw and saw no difference in them. He scanned the fence up and down the pasture and all of them were the same. Maybe it was too early, he thought? He had never tried to cross this early. He tried the section of fence to the right and left of the spot with no success. Jerry began to panic and it felt like everything was closing in. It was gone. Thoughts of Dirk and Penny flooded his mind and now the paranoia started to set in. If Dirk goes missing now, he'll get blamed for it. Nobody will believe the story he would tell of magical places and a ghost of Penny Myers. They would lock him up in the mental home with Michael and throw away the key. Heck, they may even blame him for Penny Myers going missing as well, he told himself.

After making a few more attempts on the fence, Jerry sat with his back against a post and stared out at the pasture while a crow quietly circled the sky above him. His eyes started to burn from the moisture of over achieving tear ducts, making the crisp lines of the landscape blur into the appearance of a child's abstract finger painting.

CHAPTER 18

Officer Blanchard from the Terrebonne Parish Sheriff's Office pulled into the shell driveway of Ken and Barbara Matherne with a heaviness on his chest. This was the second time in two years he was visiting this neighborhood on the report of a missing child. He was the lead guy on the Penny Myers case until it was handed over to NOPD, but this one was a little more personal.

Ken hadn't slept at all and was the first person on the phone to get through to the department. He was cautious with his demands about his missing son, knowing he would get some push back because of the shortened timeframe. He sat on the front porch with the weight of the world on his shoulders, but was trying to maintain composure for the sake of his wife.

The officer squeezed out of his patrol car with way too many objects protruding from his belt, removed his hat and approached the porch with caution.

"Good morning Kenny!" The officer offered in a friendly tone.

"I was hoping they would send you, Jason." Ken answered with a comforting tone of his own.

The two of them had known each other since their childhood, played sports together and graduated in the same class.

"Look Kenny, I understand it's only been less than 24 hours, but when I saw the name, I had to take the call."

"I appreciate that."

"How's Barb holding up?" He asked.

"She's very concerned, Jason. It just isn't like him to not at least call and he certainly wouldn't do this on a school night. I think he may be hurt somewhere and just can't get home or call." Kenny's voice cracked.

"Who is he hanging out with these days?" Jason asked, slowly beginning his investigation.

"His regular crew, but mostly with his best friend Jerry Davis." Kenny answered and pointed up the street.

"Isn't that Jim Davis' Boy?"

"Yes. Jerry said he and Dirk were coming back from camping on Sunday and Dirk had lost his flashlight. Dirk supposedly went back to look for it yesterday after church and didn't come back. We looked most of the evening last night and didn't see or hear anything." Kenny explained.

"I see. Kenny, everything okay around the house? Any reason why he may not wanna come home? Jason asked with caution.

"Everything is fine here, Jason. I'm telling you something happened to him. He would not miss school and he especially wouldn't miss football practice. If he is not coming home, he always calls." Kenny admitted.

"Not to get too personal buddy, but any chance of him doing any drugs?" Jason had to ask.

Kenny stood from the porch and made direct eye contact moving closer to Jason.

"There is no way in hell drugs are involved!" Kenny insisted and Jason could tell it was time to move on.

"I didn't think so Kenny, but you know I have to ask." Jason explained.

Kenny sat back down on the porch and put his face in his hands.

"We have to find him, Jason!"

"I know, Kenny. I will make a few calls and then I'm going over to the Davis' after school and talk to Jerry. Take care of yourself and Barb and I will let you know if I hear anything new." Jason assured him and headed back to his squad car.

@@@@@

The lone crow that was circling above Jerry's head drew closer to him as he sat crying with his back against the post. Its wings were spread wide and without an effort of flapping it descended slowly down through the sky like a glider being released from its tow line. It located a spot to land at the top of a large oak tree next to the fence.

Jerry tried to contain himself, but his mind raced with the consequences of what was to come. Was he being punished because he found this place and kept it a secret? He felt it was his fault Dirk was gone because he was the one that brought him there. Jerry wiped his eyes with his shirt and stared out over the pasture trying to think of a plan.

The crow moved down the tree, branch by branch, in a hopping motion until it was just above the top of the fence. Jerry was startled when the crow just above him now, cawed wildly and took flight narrowly missing his head. It flew away from where he sat, made a loop in the air and then headed right back towards him. Jerry ducked to avoid getting hit initially and wondered what this crazy bird was up to. He had seen birds act like this before when they warned others of an approaching predator, but this one was acting a little different. The crow flew low about 3 feet above the ground and seemed to be taking aim at Jerry's head as he sat next to the fence.

Screaming at the demented bird, he attempted to throw his hands up in a last-ditch effort to scare it off, but the crow stayed on course. Jerry practically laid on the ground as the crow zipped passed his head and flew through the fence. He instantly turned his eyes towards the fence to watch the bird and prepare for another attack, but it vanished on the other side. He blinked his eyes hard and tried to focus thinking maybe it looped around again, but it hadn't. It disappeared just like he and Dirk when they crossed to the other side. Excitement built up in Jerry and he turned to look at the post. Just like before, it was a different color now and he realized the gateway to the magic place had returned. Getting up to his knees, he wasted no time crawling through the fence and came to his feet on the other side. Jerry reached through the fence, grabbed his backpack and slid it onto his back. He took a quick look around, smiled and started running towards the cove.

@@@@@

Dirk stepped back from the window and realized what he needed to do.

"I have to go, Penny. I can't be late for supper."

"I need to explain something to you first." Penny said with soft eyes. "Time goes by a lot faster in here at night. I'm not sure why, but it does. It's actually Monday morning."

"What?" Dirk screamed. "Are you kidding me? My parents are gonna flip out!"

"Calm down Dirk, I have a plan." Penny assured him. "Now let's get you back to the fence as fast as we can. I sent a friend to help Jerry and he may already be on his way to meet us."

Dirk bolted up the stairs with Penny close behind and they stopped near the stump at the surface of the swamp.

"I have a surprise for you." Penny said smiling.

Before Dirk could ask, a sound above the trees caught his attention and then he saw it. A large bird like creature found an opening in the canopy of the trees and hovered just above both of their heads. The huge wings flapped wildly as it steadied itself which created a tornado of leaves on the ground in front of them. Dirk stepped back and caught himself before he fell.

"Is that a…?"

"Pterodactyl? Yes, it is, Dirk." Penny answered before he finished. "I'd like you to meet, Dax," she said, as if she was introducing a friend.

Dirk watched in amazement as Penny walked over to the prehistoric reptile and petted its beak. He remembered learning about them in school and how they weren't a bird, but a huge reptile that could fly. It was massive and scary, but amazing at the same time.

"Dax, take him to the gate as quickly as possible." Penny ordered.

Dax made a loud screeching noise, then leaned down to allow Dirk to climb on. Dirk looked at Penny like she was crazy.

"It's okay, he's tame. I trained him myself. He will take you to the gate and I will follow right behind you."

Dirk rolled his eyes and gave a nervous smile as he reached up to touch the creature. It snapped at him playfully and screeched again. Dirk laughed and stepped up onto a log to carefully climb aboard. Its huge bat-like wings provided a large place for Dirk to lay. He held onto the base of its neck and squeezed his knees together to prepare for the ride. Penny changed her form back into a crow and they all took flight raising above the trees in the direction of the fence.

CHAPTER 19

Sweat beaded on Jack Murphy's forehead as the heat from the morning sun radiated through his bedroom window and lit up his small reading area. His dirty unshaven face was visual proof of a man with little care for personal hygiene. The snoring drowned out the sound of knocking on the front door that echoed across the massive home. It was 9:30 AM and Jack was far from being awake on this Monday morning. He sat in his rocking chair with his chin down and his arms hung down between his legs and twitched on occasion. He hadn't made it to bed once again and sleeping in this chair after drinking most of the night was becoming a habit.

Dogs of various sizes were sleeping on the floors wherever they could find space and a few of them had already wandered outside to find something to eat. A hole in the floor in the laundry room provided them with a passageway in and out of the house. This was normal behavior in the Murphy home now because there was no purpose for the owner to thrive any longer. Jack had lost everything and the best part of his day waited on the porch at the front door in a brown paper sack. Like clockwork, a local delivery boy would deliver groceries twice a week and leave the bag on the front step and retrieve his cash from an envelope under the mat. Strict instructions were given to whoever delivered the groceries that Mr. Murphy was not to be disturbed. They were to drop the sack in a designated box on the porch, close the lid, take the money and leave. Deliveries were on Monday and Thursday and were promptly at 9:00 A.M. The contents were usually the same with an exception of a change in liquor on occasion.

1 case of potted meat

2 cans powdered milk

1 loaf of bread

1 box of Saltine crackers

1 container of Tang drink mix

12 bottles of coke

1 fifth of Jack Daniels whiskey.

1 carton of Marlboro cigarettes

Jack would leave a note in the envelope of cash with any of those changes and would give the boy hell if any mistakes were made.

The knocking on the door was not coming from a disobedient delivery boy, but from a gloved hand of Officer Blanchard, of the TPSO. Jason stood there patiently with his hands resting in a comfortable, but ready position. He scanned the front porch gathering information, familiarizing himself with the surroundings which was typical behavior for a police officer to always be aware of what's going on around him. He remembered this place from two years earlier when questioning Jack Murphy about Penny Myers and was shocked at how different it looked now. It was sad what happened to her, he thought and the long-lasting effects of such a tragedy were visible everywhere.

After knocking loudly for the third time, Jason moved over to a window and leaned over to safely look through the glass. It was covered in dust and he wiped some cobwebs aside to get a better look. A noise above his head caught his attention and he noticed a raccoon staring down at him from a large hole in the front fascia board.

One of the dogs that was awakened by the knocking, ran out of the back door and made his way around to the front of the house to investigate. The black and white spotted pit bull rounded the corner and started huffing under his breath at the officer trespassing on his property. Jason's hand quickly moved over to the butt of his revolver and turned to face the inquisitive dog. He barked a few times and then his hackles raised with the excitement of a stranger. Jason studied the dog and noticed its tail wagging which usually meant he wasn't a threat, but Jason stayed alert regardless.

Jason kept an eye on the dog, but moved his attention back to the door when he heard a voice on the other side.

"Who's there?" A grumpy voice inquired from behind the locked door.

"Mr. Murphy, its Officer Blanchard with the Sheriff's Office. Can I speak to you for a couple of minutes please?"

"What do ya want?" He asked in an angered tone.

"Mr. Murphy, I just have a few questions about a missing boy. Do you mind opening the door, sir? It will only take a couple of minutes."

There was a pause, then the sounds of multiple locks being released and Jason took a step back into a defensive posture. The door opened slowly and the tired weathered face of Jack Murphy peered out to confirm the identity of the officer. Jason removed his sunglasses and held the screen door open as the questions began. He held up a picture of Dirk he had obtained from the school yearbook that morning.

"Have you seen this boy, Mr. Murphy?"

Jack squinted his burning eyes that still hadn't quite adjusted to the morning light and studied the picture.

"I know the kid!" He grunted and continued. "I've chased him off my property many of times, but I haven't seen him for a while. He and that Davis kid are always together and usually up to no good."

"Yes sir, I understand." The officer agreed. "Did you see or hear anything peculiar last night, like maybe gunfire?"

Jack closed one eye and cocked his head to the side a bit.

"What are you gettin' at officer, what was your name again?" Jack asked.

"It's Officer Blanchard. Mr. Murphy, I spoke with some of the other neighbors in the area and they said they heard some gun shots last night around midnight. You know anything about that?"

"No sir, I didn't hear anything, especially no gunshots!" Jack explained.

"Okay, Mr. Murphy. Thank-you for your time." Officer Blanchard stepped back from the door while Jack raised his hand to keep the door from slamming shut. Jason turned to walk away, but stopped abruptly when he heard Jack mumble through the screen.

"I didn't see no ghost of Penny Myers neither"

Chills ran up Jason's spine and the hair on his arms pricked up at those words.

"What did you just say?" Jason said, turning back towards the house.

Jack's blurred, darkened silhouette looked menacing through the screen as Jason waited for a response.

"I said, I didn't see no ghost of Penny Myers last night!"

Jack stepped back from the doorway and slammed the old wooden door shut before Jason could speak. Dust flew up from the surface of the porch while Jason's hand instinctively returned to the butt of his revolver. He stared at the outside of the door for a second while he thought of his options. He could break the door down and interrogate the old man a little longer which would most likely lead to trouble on his end, or he could leave and chalk it up to the delusions of an old crazy man. Jason decided on the latter and would continue his investigation elsewhere. His system of eliminating people being involved was just getting started. He knew Jack Murphy wasn't going anywhere and he could return later if he needed to. Jason climbed back into his squad car and the radio squawked as soon as he sat down.

"Headquarters, Terrebonne 21?"

"Terrebonne 21, go ahead Headquarters." Jason answered.

"We have an assault with a weapon at 2345 Texas Gulf Rd."

"Acknowledge, Terrebonne 21 is in route." Jason placed the mic back on the clip and pulled the shifter down to drive.

He continued around the circular drive of the Murphy's property, followed the driveway back to Ferry Road and then on to Highway 316. He passed the Davis' house and felt some guilt about having to leave the case, but knew he would be back in the afternoon to question Jerry and hoped for some sort of a lead. He was slightly nervous about the call knowing that a domestic fight that involved a weapon was always a little un-nerving for any officer, but knowing that back up was not going to come for a while made it even worse.

Jason turned onto Company Canal Road, reviewed the standard operating procedures in his head on domestic assaults and prepared himself for the call. As he sat at the only red light in the small town of Bourg, the radio squawked with an update about the call and was now escalating into a barricaded subject and a hostage situation, something he wasn't used to in this area. Most of the people who live here were pretty straight forward and would work out their own issues before the police were called in. The last thing Jason needed was a long drawn out call that would keep him busy most of the day and into the night. He picked up the pace a bit, acknowledged the transmission from headquarters and dreaded what was playing out before him.

CHAPTER 20

Dirk held on tight as they lifted above the trees, but he still felt like he was going to fall off. The huge dinosaur flapped its wings gracefully and he was amazed at the power and strength of it. They gained altitude and as the trees became smaller Dirk smiled and squeezed a little tighter. Penny flapped her wings hard to catch up and fell in right behind them. When Dirk started to feel a little more comfortable, he leaned a little to the right and Dax responded. He leaned to the left and again Dax obeyed. Dirk adjusted his grip and pulled up on his neck and he slowed almost to a stop. He then leaned forward almost laying down.

"Faster!" He screamed.

Dax lowered his head and thrusted his wings with a massive force and instantly doubled their speed. Almost losing his grip, he quickly wrapped his arms around Dax's neck while his body lifted off and floated in the air just above its' back.

"Slow down, slow down!" Dirk managed to yell through his laughter.

Dax responded while he gathered himself and gave the next command.

"Let's go buzz his head!" Dirk said referring to Jerry who was about 100 feet below, running fast towards the cove.

Jerry had no idea what was above him and concentrated on the flattened grassy trail as he ran. He was worried sick about Dirk, but was also bursting with curiosity with what Penny wanted to show them.

As he neared the cattle guard, he picked up speed to attempt to jump over it. A feat that he and Dirk had mastered after years of bumps and bruises and the occasional twisted ankle. It wasn't the distance of eight feet that was a problem, but more so the footing before they launched themselves over. The area just in front and just beyond the guard was always cluttered with holes made from the hooves of cows while they waited on either side for the feed truck.

The body of the large flying creature casted a massive shadow over the ground where Jerry was about to make his jump making him lose his concentration for a second. As he left the ground, his right shoe stuck slightly in the mud and he was going to be way short on the landing. He flew helplessly through the air, closed his eyes and prepared for a very uncomfortable landing on the cattle guard.

"Catch him!" Dirk screamed.

Dax extended his large talons and as they clamped down around the backpack strapped to Jerry's back, he screamed while thrashing his arms and legs around.

"What the hell?" Jerry said in disbelief as he looked up to see what had a hold of him. He stared at the large underbelly of this prehistoric creature and then a familiar voice spoke to him from above it.

"Hang on Jerry, we're headed back to the fence." Dirk said as he maneuvered Dax in that direction.

Jerry reached up and held on tight to his backpack straps and watched a crow fly beside them as they descended toward the fence near the barn. He shook his head and thought only Dirk Matherne would come up with something so bizarre, but was glad to see that his friend was okay. Dax dropped Jerry softly onto the ground near the fence and then landed to allow Dirk to dismount as well. Jerry adjusted his backpack and was laughing as he watched Dirk proudly walking over to him with a smile from ear to ear.

"You like the new ride?" Dirk said referring to his new friend and mode of transportation.

"Yes, but not surprised, Dirk!" Jerry was quick to answer. "What happened to you last night? You said you were coming right back and I must tell you, your parents are worried sick. "

"I'm sure they are, but there is a lot you don't understand, Jerry."

"Well then help me understand, buddy? Where is Penny?" Jerry asked looking around.

"She's right behind you."

Jerry turned towards the barn and didn't see anything.

"Where?" He asked even more confused.

"Show him Penny!" Dirk said and smirked a little.

Jerry watched as a crow flew from the peak of the barn roof and headed straight for them.

"Oh great, not that crazy bird again." He said, getting ready to duck.

Penny flew down to them and hovered about eye level while she changed her form again. The boys shielded their eyes from the bright light illuminating in front of them and Penny appeared behind the light. Her curly blonde hair sparkled and was pulled over to the front of her left shoulder as the light dimmed enough for the boys to recognize their friend again.

"It's good to see you again, Jerry." She smiled.

"I, I didn't know you could do that." Jerry stuttered a little.

"There are a lot of things you don't know yet, Jerry." Penny explained. "Dirk has something to do and I'm sure he will need your help. You two better get back now and let his parents know he's okay. I'll be waiting for you, Dirk. I know you can figure it out."

"Wait Penny." Jerry spoke up. "What happened to the fence, there was no opening for a while?"

"Yea, sorry about that. I had to take it away for a bit. Mr. Thompson was snooping around and found it. I had to give him a little shocking experience, if you know what I mean?" Penny smiled at the boys, walked over to Dax and climbed onto his back. Within seconds, they rose above the barn and flew in the direction of the cove. The boys watched her disappear into the tree line near the bayou and Jerry was the first to speak.

"Start talking!" He said as he punched Dirk hard in the arm.

"Okay, okay, we can talk on the way home and we have to come up with something to tell my parents." Dirk said as he rubbed his arm. The boys crossed the fence and walked through the pasture towards Jerry's house and discussed what story would be most believable.

@@@@@

Jason turned off his lights and siren well before he reached the address on Texas Gulf Road and was hoping for a little more information on the call. He eased down the gravel drive to a single wide trailer surrounded by tall grass and a few old cars that obviously had not moved in a while. He already didn't like the way this looked. There was only one way into the property and nothing but woods in the back of the trailer.

Jason did a quick survey of the area and noticed a few things that bothered him. Toys riddled the yard which meant there may be kids involved and multiple broken windows on the front of the trailer proving violence was probable.

The door of the trailer was open which could mean someone could already be hiding somewhere ready to take a cheap shot at a would-be rescuer. All these thoughts ran through Jason's mind as he came to a stop in the drive and thought he had stalled as long as he could. Back up was most likely still 10 minutes out and he radioed to dispatch that he was on scene. Before he could get out of the car, a woman darted out of the trailer, jumped from the porch and headed in the direction of his squad car. She was bleeding, but Jason couldn't tell from where or how bad at first glance. She was screaming and crying hysterically about her husband with a knife. Jason exited his car rapidly and told the woman to stand by the hood of his car while he radioed for more back up and EMS.

He quickly assessed the woman for life threatening wounds while keeping most of his attention on the opened front door. Most of the cuts were minor except for one large gash across her leg which continued to bleed. The woman tried to approach Jason and he quickly diverted her back to the front of his car with a forceful command that she obeyed.

"Where is your husband?" Jason yelled over her uncontrollable crying.

"He's in the bedroom, I shot him!" The woman screamed.

"Where are the kids?" He asked again.

"They're in school!" She answered quickly, but slurred her speech.

Jason's adrenaline was in overdrive now, but he calmed himself and remembered his training. He quickly approached the woman, cuffed her and placed her in his back seat. He explained it was for her safety and at this point wasn't sure if she was the aggressor or the victim, but he was covering all his bases. He radioed to dispatch to let EMS know that one bleeding victim could be found in his squad car and he was making entry to check on another one. The radio was buzzing now with chatter from dispatch and other officers in route with a request for mutual aid from Lafourche Parish as well.

Jason removed his revolver and slowly made his way up the stairs of the dilapidated redwood porch. He held his gun close to his chest just like he was taught when entering a doorway and instantly checked his hard corner to the right and then left again.

"Police department!" Jason screamed loud enough for all the neighbors to hear and waited for a response. His breathing intensified with every step.

"Officer Blanchard with the Police Department, can you hear me?" Jason repeated the commands as he systematically made his way through the home.

"I'm back here" a muffled voice came from the back bedroom.

Jason swallowed hard, adjusted the grip on his pistol and eased down the hall towards the voice. His radio sounded off near his ear with a name of the home owner and Jason recognized it immediately. Although this residence was a new location for the subject, Jason had dealings with this guy before, but only on the other side of town.

Vinny Leblanc was well known for domestic violence and public drunkenness. He was a 35-year-old welder and pipe fitter and did most of his time offshore. The two weeks he did spend at home were usually a drunken blur where he would blow most of the money he earned on booze and end up in jail after fighting with his wife. Jason prepared himself for the worst and stepped quietly down the hall, avoiding more toys and beer bottles that littered the filthy carpeted floor.

CHAPTER 21

T he stories became more absurd as they walked home and they just couldn't come up with anything.

"What if you just say that you fell, hit your head and you just woke up?" Jerry offered as they made their trek back to the neighborhood.

"I don't think that will work and I'd end up with a hospital visit. You know how my mom is?" Dirk disagreed and continued. "I think I'm just gonna tell them that I wanted to be alone that I'm sorry I didn't tell anyone and I'll take my lumps."

"That's pretty brave. You sure you wanna do that?"

"I don't have a choice. You know I can't tell the truth about what's going on back there and it's the best option. I'll take the responsibility on this one, but Jerry we need to talk about what Penny showed me." Dirk stopped on the trail and faced him.

"What was it Dirk? What did she show you?"

Dirk swallowed hard and knew this wasn't going to be easy, but there was no other way.

"She showed me the window again when she fell off the platform and Michael was there, but there was something you didn't see. Someone else was there and saw the whole thing."

"What, who?" Jerry pleaded.

"Your brother, Mark." Dirk said carefully and prepared himself for the response.

"Bullshit! That's crazy!"

"I saw him, Jerry. He was in the woods, smoking and drinking beer watching her from a tree. When she fell, he hesitated while watching to see what Michael would do and then ran to the cove to look for her. It was too late. He searched the water for a while and then he got scared and approached Michael. He found Penny's clothes on the ground near Michael and did the only thing he could think of to protect them. Mark burned her clothes and buried them at the base of a China Ball tree. He told Michael to keep their secret, but let him take the fall when he was blamed for her disappearance."

Jerry stood there with his mouth open and Dirk noticed tears starting to flood his eyes.

"Why, why didn't he say anything?" Jerry managed to ask.

"Scared, I guess? Wouldn't you have been?" Dirk said and put his hand on Jerry's shoulder. "It's more than that Jerry, Penny is still there. Well, her remains are still there."

"Where?" Jerry begged.

"Inside the platform. The barge pulled her body under there and she hit her head again. She tried to call for help, but she was bleeding too much and then finally passed out. She laid there unconscious and quickly bled to death. There was nothing Mark could have done or anyone else for that matter. They would have never found her."

Jerry was speechless and stared at the ground while he tried to process the information.

"So, what do we do now?" Jerry asked after a slight pause in the conversation.

"The way I see it, we have two choices. One, we bring Mark back there, introduce him to Penny and he comes back and tells the truth or we don't tell Mark anything and we bring the cops back there ourselves. We can say we were rebuilding the platform and we found the remains. They can most likely figure out that it was an accident." Dirk explained.

Jerry continued to stare at the ground and wasn't sure what to say. The new information blew his mind and now the thought of his brother having any involvement in Penny's disappearance bothered him.

@@@@@

"Do you have any weapons?" Jason screamed again as he neared the doorway.

"No man, she shot me and ran off. I dropped the knife by the door. I need an ambulance!" Vinny responded while moaning in pain.

"The ambulance is on the way." Jason said and slowly peeked around the corner with his gun in the ready position. He saw Vinny sitting on the floor, leaning against the bed holding his left arm where it bled. Jason was about to turn the corner and move in closer when he felt a hand on his shoulder that startled him.

"I got ya covered, buddy." A voice whispered behind him.

Officer Bergeron had arrived on scene and took his spot to cover Jason as they entered the bedroom.

"Let me see your hands!" Jason ordered as he slowly approached Vinny and saw the knife on the floor. Vinny put his hands up and blood poured from the hole in his arm.

"She shot me man!" Vinny screamed and started to cry.

"Settle down man, you're not gonna die. You're shot in the arm!" Officer Bergeron announced with little concern and continued. "Your wife is bleeding pretty bad from you cutting her, so you're lucky that's all she shot." Jason turned him over face down on the floor and Officer Bergeron cuffed Vinny's arms behind his back.

"Thanks for the back-up, man!" Jason offered and took a deep breath.

"No problem!" Bergeron answered. "I secured the gun. It was in the front bathroom near the toilet under some bloody towels. Oh, and by the way, you can buy me lunch when we wrap this up."

"Sounds good." The two of them handled Vinny a little rougher than normal and escorted him outside to the other officers arriving on scene.

"We'll have medical look at his arm and then he's going downtown." Bergeron said as they carefully exited the deck that was falling apart.

Jason opened the back of the ambulance to check on Mrs. Leblanc and he found her in good shape sitting on the stretcher. Two medics were bandaging the laceration on her leg and had already stopped the bleeding on the others.

"Is he dead?" She asked looking up with her large, brown eyes.

"Not quite, Mrs." Jason tried to answer, but was interrupted.

"Call me, Celeste," she said and seemed to be flirting.

"You hit him in the arm and he will be fine, Mrs. Leblanc. As soon as you're done here, you're gonna have to come with me to the station for a full report. I'm sure you shot him in self-defense, right?" Jason asked, leading a little knowing the history between these two.

"Yes, it was, he went crazy when he got home because I was at the neighbor's house. He was already drunk and started hitting me and practically drug me home. I finally had enough and hit him back. That's when he grabbed the knife and started cutting me." Celeste explained and poured on the tears.

"Where did you get the gun?" Jason asked.

"It was in the nightstand, next to the dresser. I keep it there because he's gone a lot."

"How many times did you fire it?" Jason continued.

"Only once" She said lowering her eyes. "I wasn't trying to kill him, I just wanted him to stop cutting me." She paused and looked back up at Jason. "Am I going to jail?"

"Not sure yet, but we need to file a report and find out if you or he, want to press charges."

"I don't." Celeste answered, drying her face.

"I'm not surprised!" Jason interjected. "Are you guys done with her?" He asked the medics who were done bandaging and listening to the conversation.

"Yes, officer. We're done." One of them answered.

Jason assisted Celeste down the back step of the ambulance and led her over to his car. As they passed the other patrol car where Vinny sat cuffed and bleeding, a muffled voice made its way through the window.

"I love you baby! I know you didn't mean it!" Vinny yelled from inside the patrol car.

Jason rolled his eyes, placed Celeste in the backseat of his car and knew this process was going to be a total waste of his time. He made himself comfortable behind the wheel and pulled away from the scene in route to the station. He wasted no time getting to headquarters and handed off Celeste for processing. He would question her again once she was in the system. It was a tactic police used to see if the story changed. Ask the same questions twice, maybe even three times and switch off interviewers. One being a little more lenient and offering things while the other acted a little harder and threw out an occasional threat.

Jason bided his time and let Celeste settle into the interrogation room for a while. He made a cup of coffee and watched her from the other side of the two-way mirror. Her hair was long, black and feathered in the middle with bangs that hung down low, shading her already darkened eyes. The cut off jean shorts she was wearing were splattered with blood and her shirt was torn at the shoulder, exposing her dark tanned skin. He thought she was pretty, in a sad, helpless kind of way. Another tragic domestic violence case that he knew eventually would end up with one of them dead. Vinny was lucky it wasn't him this time, but next time maybe he would get the better of her. Jason acquired the information sheet on Celeste Boquet-Leblanc from the booking officer and took a quick trip to the break room. He grabbed another cup of coffee, a pack of cigarettes and entered the room with his offerings and a smile.

CHAPTER 22

The bleeding arm of Vinny Leblanc was illuminated by the overhead light in Emergency Room-B of Terrebonne General Hospital as the doctor threaded the needle back and forth through his skin.

"How many stitches will it take Doc?" Vinny asked as if he was proud of his injury.

"Only ten or eleven, son. Try to stay still." The doctor responded and rolled his eyes.

Officer Ray Bergeron and another officer entered the room as the doctor finished the last stitch.

"He gonna make it Doc?" Ray asked with a huge sarcastic tone.

The doctor didn't answer, but gave Ray a look that did.

"Vinny, I need to get a statement from you about the incident?" Ray asked as he placed his coat on the edge of the counter.

"It was an accident, sir. She didn't mean to shoot me. She just gets a little worked up sometimes." Vinny answered as he admired his wound and smiled.

"So, I guess you didn't mean to cut her several times either?" Ray snapped back.

"Well now, that was me just trying to protect myself, sir. She was going crazy and had too much to drink. I found her at the neighbor's house getting a little too friendly with him and we started arguing back at our place. She was throwing things at me and then went for the gun. The knife was there on the dresser so I grabbed it." Vinny said trying to explain his side of the story. "She was screaming and saying crazy things about her dead niece and how she saw her ghost at our place. I think she is losing her mind."

Officer Bergeron listened intently and wrote notes as Vinny spoke.

"You used a deadly weapon in a domestic battery case, you are going to do some time in jail, whether she presses charges against you or not. You will both see the judge in the morning and he will set your bail. If she wants to bail your butt out after that, it's up to her." Ray explained the procedure, but was still curious about the story.

"Does she see this ghost a lot?"

"She goes on about it every time I get home from offshore. She said she sees her standing in different places of our home dripping in water and covered in blood. I think she drinks too much when I'm gone, gets lonely and dreams this crap up." Vinny added.

"Does she even have a niece?" Ray asked and swallowed hard.

Vinny looked at his arm again and rubbed it a little as the numbing meds were wearing off.

"Yes, she does. Remember the girl who disappeared in the woods back near the Intracoastal a couple years back? That was her, little Penny Myers." Vinny said shaking his head.

"I remember, very tragic!" Ray said and instantly thought of Jason. Ray knew he was the lead on that case, but wasn't sure if Jason had made the connection.

"Get up so we can get these cuffs back on you." Ray told him as he stood from the chair grabbing his coat.

The officer cuffed Vinny's hands in the front this time feeling he wouldn't be much of a threat at this point and was being very cooperative. The three of them left the hospital and they transported Vinny back to headquarters to continue the process of booking him. Ray had some information for Jason and was excited about sharing it as soon as possible. He let the officer finish with Vinny, grabbed his own cup of coffee and knocked quietly on the door of the interrogation room.

@@@@@

Jason was getting nowhere with Celeste and he still thought he was wasting his time. She was telling the truth. Her story didn't change no matter how many times he asked. Neither one of them would press charges, but at least one or maybe both of them would spend a few nights in jail. He wrote notes and listened to the ramblings of another pitiful girl on a path of destruction that wasn't going to change course, in his opinion. Furthermore, his opinion didn't matter anyway, he thought. She would be right back in the same situation within a few days. Jason sat back in his chair and watched Celeste take another drag from the cigarette when he heard a knock on the door.

Ray opened the door and stuck his head in.

"Hey buddy, can I see you out here for a minute?"

Jason gladly rose from the chair, welcoming the break and excused himself from the room while shutting the door behind him.

"Yea buddy, what ya got? Jason asked adjusting his belt.

"Are you getting anywhere with that one?" Ray asked breaking the ice.

"Uh, no! You know those two are protecting each other and neither of them are gonna fold." Ray answered in a whisper.

"Do you know who you got in there?" Ray asked.

"What do you mean?"

"I mean do you know her full name and who she is?" Ray asked again.

"Yes, Celeste Boquet-Leblanc. Why, what's up?"

"Vinny said she has been going a little crazy lately talking about a ghost in their place. A ghost of a little girl." Ray explained.

"Yea, so. It's obvious she is a little off her rocker and always drunk." Jason agreed.

"She says the ghost is her niece, Penny Myers!"

Jason stared at Ray in disbelief, then looked through the glass at Celeste and back at Ray.

"What? Are you kidding me?" Ray couldn't believe it.

"No, I'm not kidding. That is Celeste Boquet, she is the sister of Penny's mom. She has been alienated from the family for a while now. She got tangled up with the wrong people and became addicted to drugs a few years back, then she met Vinny, had a few kids and you know the rest."

"I can't believe I didn't connect the dots on that one. I think I need to talk to her a little longer and maybe this won't be a waste of time after all? Two years ago, when I was investigating the disappearance, she was never mentioned." Jason became a little giddy, but cautious.

He thanked Ray for the information, gathered himself for a moment and re-entered the room with a new sense of urgency. He asked Celeste if she needed something to drink and offered up yet another cigarette to keep her calm. Celeste was beginning to get a little anxious and he could see her legs bouncing up and down. Jason needed her to stay calm. He eased her back into conversation with small talk about her kids, preparing her for the answers he really needed.

"Do you have any siblings, Celeste?" Jason asked with caution.

"Why, you need a date?" She responded with sarcasm.

"Not hardly. Just please try to answer the questions." Jason responded.

"Yes, I have a sister. She lives in Lafayette with her husband." She answered and turned her eyes towards the floor.

"Do you have any nephews or nieces?"

Celeste took a long drag of the Marlboro 100 and was slow to answer.

"I did have a niece. She died a while back or so they say? They never found her so to me, she's just missing, not dead." She answered as smoke blew passed Jason's head and joined the cloud starting to build at the ceiling.

"Is her name Penny? Penny Myers?" Jason asked to confirm.

"Yes, Penny."

She took another hit and went into a trancelike stare towards the corner of the room. He was losing her so Jason chose his next words carefully, but he needed to know. He thought back to what old man Murphy said to him on the porch earlier that morning. How was it possible that two different people were seeing the same ghost?

"Do you still see Penny?" He asked.

Celeste stared at the same corner, took another long drag and then looked right through Jason with her lip quivering when she answered.

"Yes, I've seen her a lot lately. In my living room, in my bedroom. I've even seen her standing in my bathtub. She's wearing only underwear, soaking wet and her hair is stained and dripping in blood. I see her so much I'm not even scared anymore. I think she's trying to tell me something." She explained.

Jason had more questions, but didn't want to interrupt.

"She didn't drown." Celeste continued. "The girl had gills and could swim circles around anyone. To be honest, I think that mental kid did something to her and he knows where she is. Maybe that's what she's trying to tell me by coming here?"

"Maybe?" Jason agreed.

"Well, I'll ask her next time I see her." Celeste said while lighting another cigarette from the end of the one she was finishing up.

Jason paused for a second and then stood from the table.

"I think we are done here. Someone will be here to get you and finish up the paperwork. Is there anything else I can get you?"

"A drink would be nice? Tall Vodka on the rocks with a splash of cranberry." Celeste asked, but knew what the answer would be.

"Huh, I don't think so sweetheart!" Jason laughed. "If you go home tonight or tomorrow, don't leave town. I may have some more questions about your niece."

"Sweetheart? I'll answer anything you want if you keep calling me that." Celeste was flirting again.

Jason smiled, grabbed his keys from the table and left the room. With the new information, he just received from Celeste about a ghost visiting more than one person, he needed to talk to Jerry Davis. Jason wasn't a big believer in ghosts or the afterlife, but was willing to keep an open mind if it led to something positive with the case. He still battled with never finding Penny and any information would be good information.

Jerry was the last person to see Dirk and Jason wanted to see what state of mind Dirk was in when he left. It was 2:00 PM and he knew the kids were still in school and then Jerry would be at football practice until 4:00. He thought he may visit the school and ask a few questions there first, then head over to the Davis' later when his parents were home. He needed their permission anyway. Jason met with his Lieutenant to get him up to speed with the Leblanc situation and headed back out to the school.

CHAPTER 23

The boys rounded the corner of the fence and went through the gate at Jerry's house. They stooped low as they ran through the yard, to avoid being seen by the nosey neighbors and snuck in through the back door of the house before Red heard them coming. The boys raided the refrigerator and met back at the table to secure the plan. It had to make sense and it had to be soon. Dirk knew his parents were overly concerned at this point, but would be furious when he told them his excuse. He hoped they would believe it, but knew he would be punished for it.

They decided on the combination of the two plans would be best. They would bring Mark back there first and introduce him to Penny. He needed to understand why he should have said something. Then, they would bring the cops and show them where they found Penny. They would leave it up to the Police to investigate and if they couldn't prove it was an accident, they would pressure Mark to tell the truth so Michael would be released. That was the plan anyway. They each ate a ham sandwich and pounded a few glasses of Tang before Dirk started a very short, but long walk home.

@@@@@

Jason pulled up to the Eastside Junior High School and parked out front in the bus lane. The bell for 5th period had just rung and gaggles of screaming kids were scattered about frantically moving to their next class. The presence of the police car attracted the attention of a few of them and the antics began.

"Oh, someone's going to jail?" One of the students cackled.

"Hey, he's right here, officer!" Another one joked and pointed at his buddy and pushed him.

Jason ignored the comments and followed the wide sidewalk to a glass door that read office. The administrative secretary sat at a lone desk just behind the front desk that separated the large office. She looked up from her paperwork and was quick to assist when she saw a good-looking police officer walking up. Jason was tall at 6'4" and towered above the desk and the other kids standing there. He knew it was the uniform that attracted her attention, but it still made him feel good.

"Can I help you, officer?" The secretary offered, flirting somewhat and met him at the front desk.

"I need to get some information on a student?" He paused as he noticed the other kids standing there waiting to hear a name. He smiled and slid a small piece of paper across the desk to her with the name, Dirk Matherne. Jason removed his sunglasses, gave the nosey kids a look that only a police officer can give and they went about their business. The secretary read the note, smiled back at him and was quick with an answer.

"Sure thing, what do you need to know?"

"Is there any way I could take a peek at his file? While you're in there, I also need a file on Jerry Davis as well? Jason almost whispered.

The secretary leaned in close and whispered back.

"Are they in some kind of trouble, officer? I know both of them and their parents. They seem to be pretty good kids."

"Oh, no they are fine. I'm just following up on some information for an old case and please call me Jason." He offered in a friendly tone.

"Funny you should ask? They are both absent today, Jason." She added, blushing.

"Really? The Davis boy is absent as well huh?" He laughed a little.

"I'll go get the files." She said.

"I'll wait here." Jason responded, flirting a little himself and then watched her walk away into a back office. She returned with the files and offered a desk in another empty office for Jason to review them.

"Thank you." He said sitting at the desk and starting with Dirk's file. Nothing too out of the normal was evident. The occasional sick day and one fight that led to full day of detention. No medical issues were noted or prescriptions. He seemed like a normal kid and stayed out of trouble for the most part. Opening and reading Jerry's file returned the same results, no major issues and he also looked like a good kid. Jason closed the folders and leaned back in the chair. He wasn't sure what the files would offer him, but he wanted to look anyway. Jason left the room and had one more question for the secretary before he left.

"Is it normal for the school to call the home when a kid is out sick?" Jason asked.

"Yes, I called both homes this morning. No answer at either one. I called Mrs. Davis at the school where she works and she didn't seem too concerned that Jerry wasn't answering. She said he was sick with a fever and most likely sleeping."

"I see." Jason acknowledged. "Well, thank you for your time. If I have any more questions, I'll give you a call." Jason said as he slid his sunglasses back over his eyes.

"I'll be here." The secretary smiled and watched Jason walk out of the door down the sidewalk towards his car. Her smile expanded past the corners of her mouth as she daydreamed a little and bit her lower lip.

"Another missed opportunity," she said under her breath while returning to her desk.

@@@@@

The front door of the Matherne house flew open as Barbara ran out to greet her son who was shuffling up the driveway. Ken made his way to the door when he heard Barbara screaming. She embraced Dirk at the end of the carport and the barrage of questions ensued.

"Where in the hell have you been?" She asked through uncontrollable sobbing.

"I'm sorry, Mom! I'm okay! Dirk answered trying to reassure her. He hugged her and saw the look on his Dad's face in the background. He could tell this was not going to be a pleasant experience.

"I was in the woods. I needed to be alone and I'm sorry I didn't tell anyone." Dirk said and gave his best effort.

"Are you okay?" She continued to cry as she looked her son over.

"I'm fine, Mom!" He answered again and the eased over to his Dad trying not to make eye contact.

Ken looked at him and although he was furious with his son, he was elated to see him. He grabbed him and held him tight and the anger overtook him.

"What were you thinking, son? Are you on drugs?" His dad grabbed him hard by the shoulders and demanded and answer.

"No, Dad. I'm not on drugs. I just needed to be alone." Dirk answered and searched his brain for more information to use.

"Do you realize what you have put me and your mom through? The cops have been here and they are looking for you. Where were you? The Davises and I searched the woods everywhere for you." Ken explained.

Dirk racked his brain and he felt his story and excuse was weakening so he played his final card and hoped he could pull it off.

"I wasn't in the woods, I walked to the school to meet someone." Dirk lied.

"The school? Both of his parents asked in unison.

"That's three miles from here. Who in the heck did you meet there? Ken demanded.

"A girl" Dirk answered and turned eyes his towards his dad.

"What girl?"

"Becky Smith. I met her and some of her friends at the baseball field. We hung out and played chase 'til about 8:00 and then they went home. I laid down on the bench to rest for a few minutes before I started to walk back and I fell asleep. I'm sorry!" Dirk explained and held his breath.

Ken sighed, lightened up some realizing his boy was growing up and he sympathized a little. He looked at Barbara and grinned while Dirk stared at the ground and then responded.

"Son, if you ever pull a stunt like that again, you won't sit down for a week. You're not too old to get a good whooping. Do you understand?"

"Yes sir" Dirk answered.

"Also, you're not done apologizing. You're gonna speak to Mr. Davis and the police officer who wasted his time coming out here. "I'm also going to call your coach and make sure you run extra laps for missing practice. Do I make myself clear?" Ken stressed.

"Yes sir!" Dirk put his head down and quietly entered the house and felt bad for lying, but felt good about the outcome. The extra laps were not gonna be fun and the apologies would suck, but the secret was still safe. He and Jerry's plan was working and the next move was to get Mark back there to meet Penny and then lead the cops to the cove to show them where her remains were. He went into his room, laid on his back in bed and tossed his football towards the ceiling. He would wait to hear from Jerry and let the dust settle for a while. The events of the day and the lost time throughout the night was catching up to him. He caught the ball one last time, tucked it under his arm and drifted off to sleep.

CHAPTER 24

Kenny called the police department to let them know that Dirk was back home and safe. He thanked them for their quick response. He also added that Officer Blanchard was very professional, courteous and that he should be notified immediately.

Standing at the door of Dirk's bedroom, he watched his son sleeping, fully dressed and still holding onto the football. He felt relieved and thanked God for his safe return. He made his way outside to the porch and sat with Barbara on the swing to discuss the punishment they would impose.

"What do you think we should do?" Barbara asked as she sipped from a glass of lemonade.

"I'm not sure yet. If that's what really happened, I can't really fault him." Kenny looked at Barbara with softer eyes. "Come on baby, you remember some of the crazy things we used to do? I think apologizing to the officer and the extra laps will be enough of a punishment."

"Agreed." Barbara said blushing and remembering as well. "Whatever he did, it sure took it out of him. He's out cold."

"Yes, he is. I'll let him sleep for a while and get him up before dinner." Kenny added and stepped to the end of the porch. He looked out over the front yard and watched the first of three busses that would drop off some of their children, stop at the edge of his drive. The bus door opened and their youngest boy, Johnny ran to the porch with a lunchbox in one hand and a drawing that he was obviously proud of in the other. He handed it to Kenny and joined his mother on the swing.

"How was school?" Barbara asked.

"It was fine." He answered.

"We have some great news." She said as she put her arm around him.

"What?"

Kenny turned towards them and spoke.

"Your brother, Dirk came home today. He's fine and sleeping inside so be quiet when you go in."

Johnny smiled and agreed that this was good news and he was excited to see his brother. He entered the house quietly as instructed and stopped at the bedroom door. Johnny watched his brother as he slept and wanted him to wake up to hear the story. Soon boredom overtook him and returned to the kitchen for an afternoon snack. He made himself a peanut butter and jelly sandwich and plopped down in his Dad's recliner to enjoy his afternoon ritual episode of Gilligan's island.

@@@@@

Officer Blanchard drove his squad car into the small town of Bourg on his way to the Davis' and turned left onto Company Canal road. He drove just under the speed limit and glanced occasionally at the canal that followed the road. He often thought of the way roads followed the canals in South Louisiana and wondered why. Maybe the people in the area stayed close to the water because it provided food and a place to clean up, he thought. Also, bridges were everywhere that helped connect the small cities, but always seemed to be opened more for boat traffic than cars. He noticed a few trott lines close to the edge and remembered making a few of them himself as a kid. His dad had taught him how to do it. He would put twine between two posts and then more twine with hooks and bait to catch fish. It was an easy way to catch dinner without sitting and waiting all day and was always exciting to him because you never knew what would be on the hooks.

That memory faded quickly when thoughts of Dirk Matherne crept back in and he hoped that any information from Jerry Davis would help. Jason didn't have any kids of his own, but could relate to what losing a child would feel like. He remembered the faces of Mr. and Mrs. Myers after the news of Penny and that vision still haunted him. He reached up and turned his music down when he heard his car designation from the dispatcher come over the radio.

"Headquarters, Terrebonne 21?"

"This is Terrebonne 21, go ahead headquarters." Jason answered.

"Terrebonne 21, call dispatch as soon as possible." The dispatcher requested.

Jason squeezed the microphone in response.

"Acknowledge that!"

Jason turned around in the nearest driveway and headed back towards Hebert's gas station to use the only pay phone in town. He searched for a dime in the ashtray of his cruiser and found one among the dirty change.

"Hey, this is 21, what's up?"

A young female voice responded on the other end.

"Just wanted to let you know your subject on Ferry road that was missing is now home and safe. We received a call from his father a few minutes ago."

"Did he mention where he was?" Jason asked.

"No sir, no specifics. He just said that he was home and had some great things to say about you." She mentioned with a slight chuckle.

"Well, that's great news. Maybe I'll pay them a visit."

Jason hung up the phone and headed back towards the neighborhood on Ferry road. Within a few minutes, he passed the Davis home and went a little further to the Matherne residence at the end of road. He turned down the driveway and approached the house. He found Ken and Barbara Matherne sitting on the swing smiling and Ken stood to greet him.

"I heard the good news and thought I would stop in and see you in person." Jason said with a crooked grin.

"Yes, it is great news. He's inside sleeping." Ken agreed.

"I can't wait to hear this story?" Jason laughed.

"You wouldn't believe me if I told you." Ken offered.

"Try me?"

"He was with a girl at the school baseball field. He fell asleep in the dugout. When he woke up it was 6:00 in the morning and then walked home."

"Do you believe that story?" Jason doubted him.

"I really have no reason not to. He's a good kid, Jason. He just made a mistake. I've already told him he will apologize to you and the football coach." Kenny said and offered Jason a cold soda. Jason accepted the offer and sat a few minutes with his friends. It wasn't long before the dispatcher called and Jason was off to another call about a stolen lawnmower.

He left the neighborhood and passed the Davis home on the way out where he saw Jerry sitting on the front porch. He raised a hand to wave at Jason and the officer reciprocated with a chirp of the siren. Jason was looking forward to questioning Jerry and wasn't totally convinced that the story Dirk told was the truth. The interview would be a moot point now. All that mattered was that Dirk was okay and home safe. Jason radioed headquarters to get more information on the lawnmower call and was glad it was most likely his last call of the day. From the rear-view mirror of his squad car, he watched the evening sun setting behind a row of cypress trees and he smiled knowing that he was nearing the end of a very successful shift.

CHAPTER 25

irk awoke to the aroma of fried fish that entered his room without knocking and he didn't feel rested. As a matter of fact, he felt like a zombie as he rolled over to collect his thoughts. He knew he was home because there was no mistaking the smell of his mom's fish. He even picked up on a hint of white beans which always seemed to accompany the meal. In the distance, he could hear mumbled conversations at the table as Johnny and the other siblings were finishing up their homework before supper.

When the feelings in his arms and hands returned, he gripped the football that he had slept with a little tighter and stared at the ceiling. The thought of Penny came to him again and although he was nervous about the days to come, he knew he had to follow through. Saturday would be the first chance to get Mark to the cove and that was only if they could convince him to go. He and Jerry would have to make up something intriguing to get Mark to go alone.

It was going to be a long week and he knew the consequences of his latest actions were not going to be enjoyable. An emptiness and growling from his stomach motivated him to move so he rolled out of bed in route to the kitchen. Dirk knew the ribbing from his siblings would begin as soon as he sat down, so he prepared himself. His older sister Tammy was the first to start.

"How was your nap, lover boy?" She snickered as she helped set the table. Dirk rolled his eyes, didn't answer and threw his football over to the couch in a perfect spiral.

"So, how's Becky Smith?" Tammy continued to ridicule. "Isn't she much older than you?"

Dirk didn't answer. He shoveled in some fish and white beans, like he hadn't eaten in a week. He wanted to finish and then go straight to bed again. Saturday couldn't get here fast enough, he thought and the quicker he went to sleep the sooner it would happen. Once Mark understood and the resolution of Penny's disappearance was complete, he could get back to his normal routine. Dirk finished dinner, grabbed his football from the couch and fell back into his bed for a long restfull sleep.

@@@@@

As usual, Jerry was sitting in the last seat on the bus when Dirk boarded and made his way back to join him. They gave each other a subtle grin and Jerry moved his notebook so he could sit next to him. The driver carefully turned the bus around at the end of Ferry road and headed back out towards Highway 316 to finish the route on the way to school.

News traveled fast in the small town, and even faster in the neighborhood. Stares from kids as they entered the bus towards Dirk and Jerry was proof of that. Jerry stared out the window, watched the grass on side of the road pass by in a blur and was the first to speak up.

"How did it go last night?"

"Fine. They weren't buying it at first so I switched gears and told them I was with Becky at the ball field and fell asleep."

Jerry's eyes widened and he couldn't hold in his laugh.

"Brilliant!" He said.

"Yea, well, I still have to apologize to everyone and I'm sure I'll get laps after practice today." Dirk added.

"That's okay, I'll run them with ya!" Jerry continued to laugh.

"So, what's our plan for Saturday?" Dirk asked quietly.

Jerry's eyes turned back towards the window as if looking for an answer outside the bus.

"I'm still working on that." He whispered.

They continued to talk on the way to school, but changed the subject as the bus filled with more kids. They had four days to come up with something and the hardest part was going to be the wait.

@@@@@

As expected the laps weren't very enjoyable for Dirk, but he did appreciate the company from Jerry. Dirk promised he wouldn't miss another practice and was happy it wouldn't affect his playing time. They were once again victorious on their Junior Varsity game on Thursday, beating Vandebilt Catholic by a score of 35-14. Jerry boasted about his two interceptions while Dirk was quick to remind him of his three touchdowns.

It was Friday night now and they were preparing themselves for another varsity football game from the highest point of the bleachers. However, as the fans were cheering their teams, the boys were planning their next move. How to get Mark to the cove alone? Dirk thought they should lure him with a story of a girl skinny dipping, but also thought it may scare up memories of what he had witnessed. Jerry's idea seemed to be a little more feasible. The boys would fabricate a story of finding something buried near the cove and wanted his opinion of what to do with it. That would at least get him through the fence. After that, the magic and fascination of the other side would get him to the cove. They both agreed this was the best plan and decided to plant the seed at half-time.

Dirk and Jerry stood on the long aluminum bench seat at the very top of the bleachers and watched Mark and Duke down below working hard on a group of girls. They had no interest in the game and Dirk and Jerry watched them and laughed as they crashed and burned.

The buzzer sounded for half-time and the crowd started to move towards the concessions in a safe, but hurried manner. Dirk and Jerry hugged the outside rail and jumped from seat to seat all the way to the bottom. They had neither the time nor patience to use the crowded stairs. They would need to talk to Mark alone so they needed a quick distraction for Duke.

"You're gonna have to take one for the team Dirk." Jerry said.

"What do you mean?"

"I need Mark alone for a few minutes. Can you distract Duke?"

"I can try!"

"What are you gonna do?"

"I'll think of something. You just make sure you handle your end."

"Let's do this!"

Dirk snuck through the crowd and positioned himself behind Duke as he was pushing his way through the mass of people. He waited until he was lined up with a clear path to run and went for it. With one hand, he raised Duke's t-shirt to locate his underwear and with the other, he grabbed the top of it and pulled it up as hard as he could. Duke swung around in an instant with his arm and Dirk ducked to miss it, then scampered down an open path that led beneath the bleachers.

"What the?" Duke reacted and then made chase after Dirk into the dark.

The noise and excitement of the crowd drowned out the incident and Jerry approached Mark from the front.

"What's up brat?" Mark greeted with a smirk.

"Hey, can I talk to you for a minute, I have something really important to tell you?"

"Yea, what's that?" He said as he moved out of the way of the foot traffic. "You finally gonna admit you're in love with Dirk?" He said laughing and turned to look for Duke's approval of his joke. Mark raised an eyebrow when he noticed he was gone. He looked through the crowd for Duke while he half way listened to his little brother.

"Dirk and I found something buried out by the cove and we wanted to show it to you."

Mark's eyes narrowed and he stuttered with an answer.

"Wha, what did you find?" Mark asked nervously, remembering that he had buried Penny's burnt clothes.

Jerry paused and pulled Mark under an opening in the bleachers. Sweat started to bead on Mark's forehead and he felt nauseated. Jerry let him squirm for a few seconds and then let him off the hook.

"We found a box with money in it!"

"How much money?"

"A bunch!" Jerry looked over his shoulder and then leaned in closer. "It looks like there's thousands of dollars in it. We saw it sticking up out of the mud when a barge passed by so we marked it with a jug and dug it out at low tide."

"Where is it now?"

"We hid it in a stump, but we are thinking about burying it until we figure out what to do with it." Jerry explained. "Can you help us with it tomorrow?"

"Only if I get a cut of it!" Mark answered with a huge smile.

"Okay, we are leaving early in the morning. We can tell mom and dad we are going to collect moss for Halloween."

Jerry finished speaking and turned away in a hurry.

"Where are you going?" Mark screamed.

"To help Dirk, I think he may need me!"

CHAPTER 26

Mark looked at the two of them while standing next to the fence and was curious about what they were up to. He agreed to walk with Jerry and Dirk to the back pasture, but was cautiously thinking he was being set up for something. He thought maybe they were trying to get him back for attempting to scare them.

"Okay, now what? Ya'll said you had a box full of money to show me. Where is it?" Mark asked in a sarcastic tone.

"Step through the fence" Jerry said as he held one wire up with his hand and the other down with his foot.

Mark looked at Jerry with a threatening demeanor and warned him again.

"I mean it Jerry, you better not be trying something stupid".

"Just step through, you'll understand once you step through!" Jerry said again

Mark cautiously stepped through to the other side and was instantly mesmerized.

"Woah, what just happened?" Mark questioned as he studied his surroundings.

The sky was a stunning blue with bright sunlight blasting through white puffy clouds, totally different from the gray, cooler surroundings he had just stepped from. Dirk and Jerry quickly popped through the fence to join him and Jerry watched his brother as he took it all in. Mark stared at the sky and admired the vivid colors of a distant rainbow and couldn't believe it. He turned and looked at the fence that seemed to go on forever in both directions and then disappeared beyond a hill. Tall grass swayed back and forth across the pasture and bright green thistle plants grew sporadically throughout it. He walked over to one and gazed at the pretty, purple flower that adorned the top of it. Two large black and yellow bumblebees flew in what seemed to be a choreographed pattern of pollination. Mark stared at them and the sounds of their wings were amplified in his head. The buzzing was so loud that he covered his ears and turned towards Jerry smiling. Jerry was mouthing something and then the buzzing went away.

"What?" Marked screamed while laughing.

"I said, are you ready to see more?" Jerry asked.

"Yes, yes, let's go!" Mark answered smiling wildly.

He followed Jerry and Dirk down the road, past the cattle guard and they eventually made it to the trees.

"This is so weird. How did y'all find this place?" Mark asked.

"By accident." Jerry was the first to answer. "I found the gateway in the fence chasing after a lizard."

"He showed me a couple of weeks ago." Dirk added.

"So, what is this place?" Mark looked around trying to figure things out.

"It's the place we grew up, only very different." Jerry said and continued to walk towards the trees.

"I'd say so." Mark added and followed Jerry down the path. Dirk fell in behind the two of them and couldn't wait to see the look on Mark's face.

They made their way through the trees towards the cove and stopped at the edge of the water. Mark looked out at the cove where the platform sat and noticed how new it looked. The sunlight sparkled off the water and the reflections of the trees that surrounded it cast a perfect reflection. Jerry and Dirk watched Mark staring at the platform and his mood seemed to change. He drifted off towards the memory of Penny Myers, but was interrupted when Jerry spoke.

"Do you remember?"

Mark turned abruptly and looked at Jerry.

"Remember what?" Mark asked in a nervous tone when the memory of the cove hit him.

"Penny Myers!" Jerry said and pointed at the water. "You remember, the girl you watched fall from the platform."

Mark swallowed hard and his legs weakened a little. Nobody knew about that except for him and Michael, and Michael was locked up.

"What are you talking about? Where's the money you found?" Mark said trying to change the subject.

Dirk stepped in closer and joined the conversation.

"You know what we are talking about. You and Michael were here at the cove when she fell into the water and disappeared. Why didn't you go for help?"

"You guys are crazy!" Mark snapped back and started to walk towards the trail.

"I guess if we dig in the dirt under the China Ball tree, we won't find her burnt clothes either?" Jerry snapped.

Mark stopped on the trail, dropped his head and the air left his chest. He stared at the grass below his feet and managed to speak.

"How long have you known?"

"For a few weeks now." Dirk spoke up.

"How did you know?" Mark asked with a flood of confusion.

"Mark, we have someone we would like you to meet." Jerry offered and turned to look at the cliff of land that jutted out from the left side of the cove. The 20 - foot cliff was covered in bushes and vines and a large tree at the end of it was leaning out over the water. Years of abuse from the tides and waves from passing boats had eroded the land from beneath it. It was being held in place by a few stubborn roots that seemed to not want to lose the battle. Dirk turned to look in the direction of the tree and Mark followed suit.

Penny sat high on the back of Dax as he flapped his wings with little effort and appeared from behind the fallen tree. She steered him low above the water and the air from the force of the creature's wings disturbed the surface as they picked up speed. She pulled on his neck, flaring up just before she reached them and the large animal steadied itself on the ground between the boys. Jerry and Dirk didn't move as they were used to it, but Mark shuffled backwards and couldn't believe what he was seeing.

"What the hell is that?" He gasped.

Jerry walked up and offered a hand to Penny as she slid off Dax's back.

Mark stared at Penny and was speechless as he tried to gather himself. Penny walked over to him and as Mark saw her in full view, he recognized her.

"Mark, I'd like you to meet Penny Myers." Jerry said as they stared at each other.

"How?" Was the only word Mark could muster.

Penny smiled forgivingly at Mark and he was instantly mesmerized by her green eyes that sparkle as she spoke.

"The question isn't how, but more so why? Penny continued. "I fell that day over two years ago and have been here ever since. There was a presence here that helped me along the way."

"A presence?" Mark asked.

"Yes, someone or something helping me to understand. It told me to use my imagination, so I did. I created all of this and I can change it at any time. I can do things here, but I can't interfere too much with the other side. I can change my form and try to influence things over there, but I have limitations. I'm still learning, but I feel like I am running out of time." Penny explained.

Mark stepped closer to Penny and the guilt was weighing on him like a lead coat. He felt it for a while after the incident and it faded with time, but now after meeting her it flooded back in and he knew what he had to do. Michael had been locked up for two years and he didn't deserve it. His life had been hard enough and Mark held that baggage as well. Heaviness filled his chest and with his eyes filled with tears, he spoke.

"I'm so sorry. I will tell them what happened." Mark offered, choking on his words.

Dirk and Jerry sat on the old tree and listened as Mark and Penny had more conversation about the plan. Mark agreed to tell the police exactly what happened and they would have no choice, but to release Michael. Jerry and Dirk joined the conversation and agreed to say that they found her remains in the platform. The Myers family would have closure and they could have a proper burial for Penny.

Penny thanked them all as hugs were exchanged and she assured them everything was going to be okay. She climbed onto Dax's back and the boys watched as they lifted off the ground. Penny steered Dax towards the trees and turned to wave at the boys one last time. Suddenly, a flock of red breasted robins were startled from a tree and Dax flared up hard to avoid them, causing Penny to lose her grip. She fell 15 feet to the ground and struck her head on a partially buried rock. The boys were at her side within seconds and Dirk grabbed her shoulders and gave her a gentle shake.

"Penny, Penny, are you alright?" Dirk asked, but got no response.

"Penny?" Dirk raised his voice, wiped dirt from her forehead and gently pulled her long blonde hair back that covered her face. He moved her head slightly and noticed the blood-stained rock beneath her.

@@@@@

Dirk and Jerry sat beside each other on one side of the table across from the mysterious woman as Mr. Webb and one of his associates disseminated the paperwork so that everyone had a copy. He also made sure that everyone had their own signing pen that was clearly advertised with the firm's name on the side of them. Mr. Webb was the first to speak.

"Mr. Davis and Mr. Matherne, I'm sure you are curious to know what this is all about so I'll get right to it. I received a letter from a client naming you two gentlemen as sole recipients of a rather large settlement. The client was very specific with the terms and will be represented today by Mrs. Adams." Louis Webb pointed towards the woman in the hat and continued. "I can only assume that neither of you have discussed this meeting with anyone else besides each other. Is that correct?"

Dirk and Jerry nodded in agreement.

"If you will direct your attention to the first page in front of you, can you please verify that is the correct spelling of your names and the correct address where you presently reside?"

They both read their names and addresses and agreed.

"Now, on to page two. Can you please verify that neither of you have ever been convicted of a felony in the state of Louisiana?"

Dirk and Jerry looked at each other, laughed and both answered "NO" simultaneously.

"Perfect! Now if you will just initial the bottom of page one and two we can move on to page three."

Dirk turned the page, glanced up at Ms. Adams who seemed agitated to be there and he could feel the tension building from across the table. He immediately looked down and began to scan page three. The first number he saw had quite a few zeros and he tried to refrain from smiling. It took a few seconds, but he finally realized how much it was. Even hearing the number coming from Mr. Webb's mouth seemed surreal. He slid his hand over to Jerry's leg beneath the table and squeezed it. Jerry winced a little and desperately tried to contain himself as well. They both initialed the bottom of page 3 and turned to page 4 as instructed. Dirk's eyes finally found a name he recognized and as he read the name silently, he heard Jerry whisper her name.

"Penny Myers, well I'll be damned!"

CHAPTER 27

The two of them looked at each other and then back at the papers in unison. Behind the dark glasses, Collette's eyes studied the two men sitting across from her and was more interested in Jerry. His smile was the first thing she noticed and it seemed familiar to her. She was sure they had never met, but something kept gnawing at her. The silence in the room was deafening until Collette spoke from across the table.

"Do you mind if I say something, Mr. Webb?" Her voice was very southern and matter of fact.

"No ma'am, please go right ahead." Webb answered abruptly with a crooked smile and instantly became a little uneasy.

"Gentlemen, I am the daughter of Penny Myers. I am here because my mother feels like you two somehow deserve one half of our estate and holdings."

Dirk and Jerry became uncomfortable in their seats and they both tugged at their collars as if on cue.

"I'm not sure how you two convinced her to do this because to be quite honest, this is the first time I've heard of either one of you. Maybe one of you can explain why my mother would leave half of her fortune to two strangers? I know towards the end she was getting very confused and speaking of things that didn't make since, but it is very clear in her will that this is what she wanted. I promise, I will get to the bottom of this."

Dirk was the first to speak and he shuffled in his seat again, but no position was comfortable.

"Not to get too personal, but what kinds of things was she saying?" He asked while nervously clicking his pen.

Collette Adams lowered her sunglasses and her bright green eyes peered out from behind them as she answered.

"Nonsense is what she was saying. She spoke of magical places in the swamp and flying dinosaurs. The doctors said it's normal for cancer patients on pain meds to recall books she may have read or movies she had seen and speak as if they really happened. It's a horrible disease and she didn't deserve to go out like that!"

"I agree!" Dirk answered and continued cautiously. "We met your mom one summer here and spent time with her a few summers after that at your great uncle's farm, Mr. Murphy. It was a long time ago."

"So that's it? Ya'll spend a few summers frolicking through cow pastures and swimming in muddy water and she gives ya'll half of everything? I don't buy it! My mom assisted my grandparents in launching one of the biggest health and wellness products that this world has ever seen. She continued as the CEO when they were too old to continue and built it into a multi - million-dollar company. You two, as far as I know, had nothing to do with that and you feel like y'all deserve half? There has to be more to it than that?" Collette pulled the glasses from her face and waited for an answer. Dirk and Jerry were speechless and looked at Mr. Webb for some help.

"Look let's not get too fired up here." Mr. Webb interjected. "The fact is, the will is the last known request of Mrs. Penny Myers and whatever did or didn't happen is a moot point. It's my job to execute it as accurately and as timely as I can. Once it is signed by all parties, the funds will be dispersed. Ms. Adams, I don't mean any disrespect, but you are only here as a witness to the signatures." Collette placed her glasses back over her eyes, sat back in her chair and folded her arms.

Dirk signed the last page giving access to direct deposits as did Jerry and slid the papers back towards Mr. Webb. He collected the papers and tapped them on the table in an attempt to even them out and then he slid three separate envelopes to each of them. Each of their envelopes had their names written on them in a fancy jet black, calligraphy style.

"What's this?" Collette asked.

"These are letters written to each of you from the deceased. They are confidential and have been sealed since we received them in the mail from Mrs. Myers. We are aware of their content and be rest assured that it does not interfere with the will in any way. Are there any questions or concerns?" Webb explained in detail.

Dirk and Jerry accepted the envelopes and stared at the floor trying to avoid any eye contact coming from across the table, but Collette abruptly sat up and spoke.

"Just to be clear, there aren't any other people that may come out of the woods or bayou claiming they are entitled to any more of my money, right?" Collette directed the question to Mr. Webb, but stared at Dirk and Jerry.

"No other family members were mentioned in the will. Is there someone you are concerned about?" Webb asked.

"No, not really. However, my long, lost deadbeat father may show up thinking he deserves something." She said with a defiant and sarcastic tone.

"He wasn't mentioned so I certainly doubt it. Do you know where he is?" Webb was curious.

"No and I don't want to. My mom said he never knew me. He got her pregnant, went into the Marines before I was born and she never heard from him again. I never even knew his name, but she said the loser was from around here. We never really talked about it while I was growing up. Anyway, it doesn't matter as long as he isn't entitled to anything, I'm not worried about it."

With the mention of the Marine in the area, Jerry and Dirk cringed at the conversation. They never put it together before, but it all made since now. Mark had disappeared and then never returned home because this girl was his kid. He was running from the responsibility and staying in the Marines was his savior. Jerry started to sweat and his breathing increased as he realized the girl sitting across the table from them was his niece. Collette Adams, obviously her married name, was the daughter of Penny Myers and his brother Mark. Feeling a sickness overcoming his body, he looked over at Dirk who was staring back at him wide eyed and his mind wandered.

CHAPTER 28

The boys surrounded Penny and watched her laying there, pale and breathing fast, gasping for air at times.

"Penny?" Dirk screamed again and then his voice seemed to fade away.

She turned her head to the side and strained to hear Dirk's voice better, but the more she tried the lower it became. Darkness closed in around her eyes and she blinked.

"Penny, wake up dear! What are you doing on the floor?" Her uncle asked as he stroked her forehead.

Penny opened her eyes and was looking at her Uncle Jack with a blank stare from the cold bathroom floor. The damp wash cloth was still in her hand and her mouth was dry with an odd taste. He knelt over her with his large hat casting a shadow on her face from the light above him.

"Did you sleep here on the floor?" He asked her with a puzzled look.

Penny was speechless and could only stare at her uncle. She didn't understand. She was at the cove with the boys in the magic place. *What happened?* She thought. She looked at her Uncle Jack and noticed how good he looked. He was a far cry from the old, broken down man she visited that night in his dilapidated home. How could this be?

"Are you okay Penny?" He asked again.

The words echoed in her head as Jack helped her to her feet.

"Yes, I think so." Penny answered as she was helped over to the bed. She wasn't sure, but she could swear she heard Michael in the dining room.

"Is that Michael in there?" She asked with a wrinkled brow.

"Yes, he's eating breakfast. Getting ready to start the morning chores." Jack laughed at the question. "You up for it?"

"I guess!" Penny answered still trying to gather herself.

"Okay, get cleaned up and we will see you at breakfast."

Jack left the room and Penny scratched her head, wondering what the heck was going on. She cleaned herself up in the sink, changed her clothes and entered the dining room for breakfast. She sat at the table with her eyes directed at Michael and her aunt, almost scared to accept the present situation. She managed a smile at Michael and he smiled back at her with a mouthful of scrambled eggs.

"How's your head, sweetie? Aunt Murphy asked over her cup of coffee.

"It's fine," she answered.

"You gave us a pretty big scare yesterday." Her aunt added.

"Yes, I'm sorry about that. Do you think I could skip the chores this morning and take a walk? My head still kinda hurts."

Jack looked at Penny over the rim of his glasses and spoke.

"Are you sure you're okay? You're usually not one to pass on anything to do with horses, but I understand. You did take a pretty good fall yesterday. Michael and I will handle the chores, but after lunch we will go for a ride. You need to get back on Max as soon as possible."

"I understand, sir." Penny assured.

She finished her breakfast and headed towards the fence at the back of the property. Her mind was reeling about what was happening. Could it all have been a dream? That scenario seemed impossible. Everything was so real and she felt things like she had never experienced before. It had to be real, she thought. As soon as she was over the fence, she ran as fast as she could to the cove. She slowed at the edge of the trees, gasping for air and followed a flattened path of grass to the other side. She could hear voices as she approached the cove and she stopped just before the opening behind a tree. Moving her eyes around the curvature of the tree, she saw two boys standing at the edge of the bayou. It was Jerry and Dirk. They were skipping rocks out into the cove and laughing at each other's lack of performance. Penny moved from behind the tree and quietly walked up behind them.

"Hello boys!" Penny said.

Dirk and Jerry swung around simultaneously and was shocked to see a girl standing behind them. They knew every girl in the neighborhood and they surely had never seen this one. Especially back here in their secret spot. They didn't recognize her from school either. She was pretty, Dirk thought. She wore cut off jean shorts and a 1/2 cut t-shirt with a rock band patch on the front. Her long blonde curly hair was feathered and flowed slightly in the wind. A scent of her perfume blew in the breeze past the boys and they enjoyed the nice smell which rarely visited their hideaway. Penny smiled at them purposely, like when a person smiles at someone they know. The boys looked at each other and then back at her to make sure they weren't dreaming. Jerry nudged Dirk with an elbow encouraging him to make the first move.

"Uh, hello." Dirk said blushing.

"It's so great to see you two again." Penny said.

The boys looked at each other confused.

"Again?" They asked in unison.

"Have we met before?" Dirk asked.

"Guys, it's me Penny! Penny Myers!" She said raising her palms and wrinkling her nose.

They studied her face and tried to remember anything about her, but nothing came to them.

"Are you sure we've met?" Jerry spoke this time.

Penny's face changed and now she was confused. She walked towards them and looked past them into the cove.

"Where's the platform?" She asked and pointed out to the water.

The boys looked at each other for the third time.

"How do you know about the platform? Dirk asked and continued. Our parents made us take it down after the accident. What did you say your name was again?"

Penny stared out at the water with a dazed look on her face.

"What accident?" She dared to ask.

"My brother, Mark fell off it and broke his arm on a sunken tree.

"When?" She muttered.

"Last week!" Jerry popped off.

"No, I fell off! I hit my head and I was stuck under it. Remember?" She spoke as she relived the incident. "Michael saw it and your brother Mark was here." She pointed at Jerry.

"Are you okay?" Jerry asked and stepped closer.

Penny looked at them like they were crazy and questioned.

"Are you telling me this was all a dream?"

"I'm sorry, but we've never seen you before." Dirk said and Jerry agreed shaking his head.

"Then how do I know so much about you?" Penny added.

The boys stood there with puzzled looks.

"What do you know about us?" Dirk spoke up.

"I know that both of you play football. I know that you have a place dug into the muddy bank where y'all hide from Mark and your other brothers. I know that Dirk thinks Becky Smith is the prettiest girl in school. I know that you, Jerry will break your leg at the first practice this fall and I bet you a hundred dollars you have a slingshot in your bag."

Jerry and Dirk stood there amazed, but confused at the same time and neither could speak. How could she know this? They were sure they had never seen her before.

Jerry reached down, picked up his bag and slowly pulled out the sling shot.

"I told you!" Penny bragged.

Penny sat down and the boys joined her on a small grassy area next to the bayou and for the next two hours, Penny filled in the blanks. The boys listened intently while Penny tried to lay it all out. She told of her accident and how Michael was sent away with Mark keeping his silence. She knew of their parents, their siblings and answered every question they had with scary accuracy.

She explained the magic world she created and the gateway through the fence. They laughed hysterically about flying on Dax and Mark wearing a dress. She told them about everything they did and how she watched them make certain decisions, good and bad. When she was finished, she rose from the grass, looked towards the water and her voice softened.

"I'm not sure why or how this came to be, but I do know that it was real, I'm alive and I thank you for being a part of it. I've learned so much from all of this! I'm sure you both understand that this should be kept just between us?" Penny finished.

"I don't think that will be a problem. Who's gonna believe us anyway?" Dirk smiled.

"What about Mark?" Jerry asked.

Penny smiled and continued.

"I haven't met Mark yet, so he knows nothing. He is most likely getting ready to steal a couple of beers from your Dad, cigarettes from your Mom and will be on his way back here as planned. He will never witness me falling from the platform so some things will change." Penny continued. "I guess it already has started to change. Mark didn't have a broken arm before. You two had already left the cove that morning and went home by the time I got here to go swimming. From this point on, who knows what will happen? I'm just thrilled to be here to enjoy it."

Penny hugged both of them extra tight and told them she would see them soon. She walked away and disappeared through the trees leaving the boys confused, but very excited about things to come.

Dirk and Jerry laid on their backs in the soft grass along the bank of the bayou with their minds reeling. They decided to wait for Mark and give him a little scare as he drank a beer and lit up a cigarette. A little blackmail may come in handy later, Jerry thought. Both had their hands tucked behind their heads while chewing on a long piece of rye grass. High above them, a murder of crows circled the clear blue sky and they both smiled. The two of them took in the warmth of the sun beaming through the trees and were excited about the endless possibilities ahead of them. They discussed the decisions they would change and how it would set a new course for their lives on one side, but knew fate would be waiting for them on the other.

CHAPTER 29

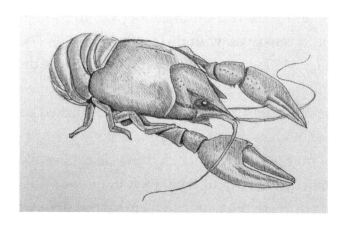

Just like Penny told them, Mark appeared on the horizon across the pasture headed towards the cove. He was easy to spot with one arm swinging back and forth and the other in a sling and cast. The fall from the platform had broken his upper arm and he tore cartilage in his throwing arm. He would be out for the baseball season this year and hope to rehab and help out where he could. Mr. Davis wasn't happy about it, but felt lucky it wasn't worse. The platform came down just as quickly as it went up and they were given strict orders not to build another one.

As Mark approached the edge of the woods, Jerry and Dirk found a fallen tree to hide behind and waited for the right moment. They watched over the top of it through a thicket of blackberry vines and kudzu while Mark sat with his back against a large oak looking out over the canal. Looking over both shoulders, he scanned the area making sure he was alone. He reached into the left pocket of his steel blue Members Only jacket and retrieved a cigarette and lighter. Blocking the wind with his sling, he took two long drags as he lit the end. He inhaled deeply and the boys giggled quietly as Mark released the smoke from his nose. A trick he had learned from Duke under the football stadium a few years prior. After a few puffs, he reached into his left pocket again and pulled a small Miller Lite beer bottle from it and twisted the top off with the fingers of his casted hand. Smoking and drinking wasn't a habit yet for Mark, but was just something to pass the time and look cool amongst his peers. He pinched the beer cap between his finger and thumb and with an effortless snap, it sailed through the air and landed about fifteen feet out into the water. He smiled at his small accomplishment and took a long sip from the warm beer.

Jerry and Dirk sat watching for a few minutes and then felt it was time. They both jumped up from behind the tree which was only about thirty feet behind Mark and screamed.

"Hey, whatcha doing?" They managed to yell while they watched Mark jump and turn to see them.

He instinctively flicked what was left of his cigarette quickly into the water and slowly slid the beer into his jacket pocket as he stood.

"It's too late, we saw what you were doing." Jerry was quick with the accusation.

"Oh yea, what did you see?"

"We both saw you smoking and drinking a beer."

"No, you didn't."

"Yes, we did. You flicked the cigarette into the water and the beer is in your pocket."

"So, what are you gonna do, tell mom and dad? I'll kick your butt and yours too, Dirk, if you say anything." Mark warned.

"No, we won't tell, yet. I think I'll hold this card for a while." Jerry smiled.

"Whatever!" Mark turned back towards the water and pulled the beer from his pocket. He took another long sip and finished it. He gripped the bottle in his left hand and threw it as far as he could, but it barely made it to the water.

"Not so good with the left arm, are ya Mark?" Dirk teased, but regretted it immediately when Mark gave him a look that would kill.

"Don't y'all have something better to do than bother me?"

"Yep, we were just leaving. We have a pickup game at the school." Jerry bragged.

"Great, you two have fun. Try not to break anything." Mark said as he raised his casted arm in the sling and then sat down against the tree again.

Dirk and Jerry left the cove and headed back to the neighborhood looking forward to the football game and argued the whole way back about who would be the quarterback.

@@@@@

Rays of sunlight penetrated through the falling leaves of the massive oak tree as the wind blew slightly, moving the smaller branches with ease. The warmth felt good on Mark's face as he closed his eyes and turned his cheeks towards the sky to soak it in. He peeked out on occasion to admire the majestic tree above him as it swayed and adapted to its environment. He had climbed it many times and though it was showing signs of age with broken and dying branches, it was still full of life and strong. Part of a rope that they had used for a swing at one time was still attached around one of the bigger branches, but had weathered and broke two summers ago. Mark recalled the day it happened and as he played it back in his head, he smiled.

Jerry was showing off to some of his friends and climbed to the highest part of the tree that day. When the swing was extended out far over the water, it broke! In the heat of the summer, lily pads would multiply across the water and cover the cove like a colored blanket of green and purple. When the rope popped, Jerry flew through the air and then he and the rope disappeared beneath the lilies. It took him a few seconds to find his way back up through them only to hear the roar of laughter coming from the land. Jerry bore the nickname of Lilly for quite a while after that.

Time passed quickly as Mark sat there reminiscing about the good times they had in the cove and the light was diminishing beyond the trees. His attention was captured near the water as a crawfish was working feverishly on its home. Like a bricklayer at work, it meticulously deposited small mud pellets side by side in the formation of a muddy chimney surrounding its' hole. Some say it was for protection as it moved mud from the hole and others argued that it helped with airflow into the water filled hole. Either way, Mark was transfixed on it like a micro-managing foreman at a job site with a hundred and eighty-day safety streak.

He was abruptly startled by the sound of a twig snapping behind him and he whipped his head around to see a girl standing there. She was pretty, he thought and definitely not from around there. Briskly standing up, he brushed off a few dead leaves that had attached themselves to his pants and ran his free hand through his feathered black hair.

"Hello?" Penny offered in a slow soft tone.

"Hi!" Mark responded smiling, slipped his casted hand from its sling and offered a handshake.

"I'm Mark Davis. It's a pleasure to meet you." He held her hand a little too long and was instantly captivated by her glowing green eyes and beautiful smile.

CHAPTER 30

irk and Jerry quickly stood from the table with each of their envelopes in hand and couldn't wait to read them. Jerry offered his hand towards Collette and she shook it with a firm, but uninterested grip. Dirk gave her a modest smile from across the table which she responded to with a crinkled lip and head nod. Jerry felt bad about not mentioning the relationship with Collette yet, but he wanted to be absolutely sure before he said anything. They said their goodbyes and thanked Mr. Webb for orchestrating the meeting. The two of them left the office and briskly made it across the parking lot to Jerry's car. Jerry unlocked the doors with the remote long before they reached it and they were barely seated before the ripping of the paper began. They each unfolded the crisp white paper and then stopped before reading it.

"You want to read them out loud?" Jerry offered.

"Sure, you go first!" Dirk said.

Jerry smiled, stretched the papers across the steering wheel and was giddy as he began to read aloud.

"Jerry, I hope this letter finds you well and if it has, I have already moved on to the other side. I wanted to leave you with this letter and a little something to remember me by. I'm sure by now

you are severely confused about me having a child with your brother and I'm sorry about the way things happened. When I left that last summer and became pregnant, my father refused to let me return and then I spent the next 5 years in Paris. As you most likely know, now that you have met her, she is pretty stubborn and strong willed like me. It was tough raising her without a father, but I did the best I could. Please don't hold any ill will towards your brother, we were young and scared and I never expected anything from him.

Collette is very well travelled, extremely smart and now very wealthy. When she reads her letter, she will finally know the truth about her dad and her extended family. I'm not sure how she will react, so please be patient with her. I'm not sure where you are financially, but hopefully you won't have to worry about that anymore. You and Dirk were a big part of my childhood, and I'm still unsure how and why any of that took place. What I do know, is that it happened for a reason and y'all were there for me when I needed you. Y'all believed in me when nobody else did. Take care of yourself and I'll be seeing ya beyond the fence! Love always, Penny."

Jerry refolded the letter and placed it neatly back into the envelope. He glanced over at Dirk who had already started to read his letter in a mumbled tone and then spoke up.

"Mine is pretty much the same except for the niece part."

"Wow!" Is all Jerry could muster as he stared out the windshield shaking his head.

"Look, there she goes!" Dirk said as he reached over and hit Jerry in the arm.

He noticed Collette leaving the office and the large man opening the door to the SUV. She paused at the side of it for a second and turned towards them. From across the parking lot, they watched as she lowered her sunglasses, stared in their direction and smiled.

"Did you see that?" Jerry whispered.

"Yes, I did." Dirk whispered back as they both peered at the SUV. "Do you think she knows?"

"How could she? There's no way she read the letter that quick." Jerry added.

"That was weird!" Dirk said as he slipped his envelope into the pocket of his blazer.

"Very!" Jerry said as he cranked the car and eased from the lot. "Well, you wanna grab a drink somewhere?"

"Naw, I don't drink anymore sha!" Dirk said using his best Cajun accent while trying to contain his laughter.

"Yeah, you don't drink any less either!" Jerry quipped.

"I'm a little short on money, you buying?" Dirk said still trying to be funny.

The two of them broke into a childlike laughter and turned onto Main Street heading towards the closest bar.

From across the street, Mark was sitting on a Harley Davidson waiting. He wore sunglasses and an LSU baseball cap low on his head. His hair was long and the black beard that covered his face had places of gray showing his age. He stayed concealed from their view between two trucks, pulled out behind them and then followed them from a distance.

Three miles and two turns later found them in the parking lot of the Jolly Inn, a local bar and restaurant famous for their Friday night Fais-do-do, a popular Cajun dance or party originating from World War II. The phrase actually meant (go to sleep) and was used by mothers of bawling children to get them to go to sleep in a hurried manner before she found her husband dancing with another woman.

"Wow, talk about a flashback! I remember this place. I haven't been here since I left for Florida in the 80's." Dirk said smiling.

"I thought you'd like it." Jerry boasted.

The two entered the building, found a table near a window overlooking Barrow Street and ordered drinks immediately.

"You gonna eat something or just have drinks?" Jerry said perusing the laminated paper menu.

"Does it look like I miss meals?" Dirk was quick to answer rubbing his slightly bulging belly.

"I wasn't gonna say anything, but I did notice you have packed on a few pounds." Jerry joked.

"At least I have hair."

"That you do, fat boy. That you do!"

They both laughed and carried on the barrage of insults while ordering food from a waitress who didn't dare to join in on the insults.

While the two of them carried on inside, the door of Jerry's car was quietly opened and Mark ducked low to slide into the front seat. The windows were cracked about six inches to allow the muggy Louisiana heat to escape from the blistering black leather seats. Carefully surveilling the front door and making sure the view from the window was obscured, he reached onto the dash and grabbed one of the opened envelopes with Jerry's name on the front. He unfolded the page and started to read. The letter from Penny telling of her passing wasn't a surprise, however the talk of money from an estate was. He had been home for two months, but laid low and made no contact with family. He heard the story directly from Penny about falling ill when he received a letter from a Private Investigator that she had hired. He felt horrible about it, but knew it was too late to make amends now.

Mark followed Jerry and watched him from a distance for weeks. He then used an old detective friend to dig up some information on Collette. She still resided in Lafayette with her husband and had a little girl of her own. Mark followed her for a while and then broke off when she made it into town. He knew the meeting was going down, but had no idea of the particulars, until now.

"What on earth is she talking about?" Mark mumbled as he watched the front door like a hawk. "When were they there for her?"

He folded the letter back and replaced it on the dash. The curiosity of the other one overcame the fear of being caught, so he grabbed it and pulled the thick folded clump from its holder. Mark read through quickly noticing certain words and initials until the last page and he nearly choked on the spit that was collecting in the back of his throat.

"One and a half million dollars? What the hell is this? Are you frickin' kidding me?" Mark wasn't mumbling anymore and his voice carried across the parking lot to an old man washing a pot in an out kitchen behind the restaurant. It was enough to spook Mark, so he slid from the car like a snake easing through tall winter grass. He looked back at the old man staring at him and he raised a single finger to his lips while pulling his leather jacket back just far enough to reveal the butt of a revolver. The old man took the hint and went about his business washing pots. Mark mounted his bike and took off fast enough to throw broken oyster shells into the air towards Jerry's car. The commotion caught the attention of Dirk and he moved over closer to the window to get a better look.

"I guess he's in a hurry?" Dirk said as he watched the Harley pick up speed down Barrow Street.

"Idiot! He's probably drunk and will hit and kill some innocent person on their way to church." Jerry was quick to add.

"Speaking of church, you still going?" Dirk asked.

"Yup, every Sunday. I actually help with communion on occasion." Jerry boasted. "What about you?"

"Yea, me too. I go on occasion." Dirk answered, slightly ashamed.

The conversation paused for a while and after chewing the last bite of his oyster Po'boy, Dirk started.

"Do you ever wonder if Penny was actually telling the truth that day?"

Jerry took a swig of his beer and looked at the ceiling as if looking for the answer somewhere amongst the smoked stained tiles that hadn't been washed since the restaurant smoking law changed.

"Of course, I do. There isn't a day goes by that I don't think about it." Jerry tried to lower his voice. "I've been wanting to talk to you about it for a while now. The fact is, there is no way she would know all those things about us. What bothers me is all the things that changed because of that day. Do you realize how different things would be?" Jerry was getting a little amped and was having trouble containing himself. "If she had died that day, for starters, your dad would most likely still be around."

"You don't know that!" Dirk snipped.

"Oh, I don't? Do you remember what Penny said? Her uncle became a recluse, the ranch was in shambles and out of business. There would be no buying, selling or training of horses. The horse trailer that detached from the truck on

Highway 90 that killed your dad was on its way to her uncle's ranch. So, if she had died there would be no trailer."

"What are you talking about?" Dirk asked getting a little uncomfortable.

"After you left town in 88, I started questioning things. I did some digging after your dad's funeral in 92 and found that it was Murphy's trailer." Jerry explained. "That's not the only thing. Penny also said that her aunt left her Uncle Murphy and Michael was sent to the mental facility, right? Well, when that didn't happen, it initiated something else. She ended up having relations with Joe, the horse trainer and that exploded into a bad episode of Young and the Restless. When Joe was fired and Murphy hired a new trainer, he had ties in Mississippi and that's who was driving the truck."

"What? That's crazy!" Dirk shook his head in disbelief.

"You ready for this?" Jerry moved in closer. "Remember Penny said there was some kind of presence on the other side helping her?"

"Yea, I remember."

"Did you know there was a murder of a young girl back there in the early fifties?"

"No, who?" Dirk was curious now.

"A little girl named Olivia. She was 11 and one of the daughters of a family that lived and worked on the Thompson property. Back then, all of the land belonged to Erwin Thompson, the father of Paul Thompson. They found her hanging from a tree where the cove is now, before the Intracoastal was even there. The research I found was they never found her killer or maybe they did and covered it up? Either way, I'm not a big believer in spirits and ghosts, but maybe she was the one helping Penny? I found out later that the little girl's family had ties with one of the biggest Voodoo Queens in New Orleans! All of those things changed the course of our life, whether you want to believe it or not."

"Are you listening to yourself right now? Ghosts, spirits, Voodoo Queens and girls hanging in trees?" Dirk chuckled, but he could tell Jerry was serious. He could always tell when he was serious. Jerry sat back in his chair, folded his arms and stared out the window. Dirk finished his beer, stared at his friend across the table and wiped the beer froth from his upper lip, knowing that Jerry was right. They had cheated fate and so far, most things were okay, but he knew there would be a price. The question was, when would fate come to collect?

CHAPTER 31

Dirk took his last sip of beer and placed the empty glass on the table.

"So, you're telling me that you think the ghost of this girl from the fifties that was killed near the cove, helped Penny come back from the dead in some sort of time warp, Voodoo trip and is the reason everything happened like it did? Man, I'm starting to worry about you." Dirk copied Jerry's posture and waited for a response. Jerry turned his gaze back towards Dirk.

"Then how would you explain it and why in the hell would she leave us over a million dollars each? Something happened back there, I feel it in my bones. I've always felt it. You can be a non - believer all you want, but I will get to the bottom of this!" Jerry pressed.

"And just how do you plan on doing that?" Dirk laughed.

"Penny is really dead now. I think she wants us to go back there again. I think she will open the gateway again and prove to us that we aren't crazy and she was right. You read the letter, see ya beyond the fence? I think it is a hidden message to get us back there again." Jerry whispered as the waitress approached.

"Can I get you guys anything else?" She smiled, blinked her extra-long eyelashes in front of her dark brown eyes and laid the Southern charm on extra thick to try and boost her tip.

"No boo, I think we are good here. You can bring him the check." Jerry said smiling and pointing towards Dirk.

As the waitress walked away, Dirk continued quietly.

"So, what do you plan on doing?"

"I'm going back to the fence. The question is, are you brave enough to come with me?" Jerry looked at him with that same childish grin Dirk new too well practically daring him to go.

"You're serious about this aren't you?"

"You damn right I am! My brother Mike, bought our old house from my parents, did some renovations and has been there for about ten years now. We can park there and walk to the corner of the fences by the barn. I think Penny will be waiting for us." Jerry smiled.

Dirk received the check from the waitress, thought about the days ahead and decided to stay and join in the fun to fulfill his morbid curiosity.

"I'll go with you, but I'm only going so you won't feel so stupid by yourself when nothing happens. I'll do it because you're my best friend and I love you."

"Awe, you wuv me? I wuv you too big guy!" Jerry repeated it loudly just as the waitress collected dirty dishes and they all broke into laughter.

@@@@@

Jerry started the car and waited for Dirk to finish up in the bathroom of the restaurant and noticed something strange. He waited for Dirk to return before moving anything. Dirk plopped into the front seat of Jerry's Chrysler 300 and instinctively buckled his seatbelt when Jerry asked.

"Hey, did you move my envelopes from the dashboard when we got here?"

"No, I didn't touch them. Why?"

"Because I thought for sure I left them on the dash when we got here?" Jerry wrinkled his brow.

"Maybe the wind blew it down? The windows were down some." Dirk offered.

"There isn't that much wind and as thick and heavy as this one was, I don't believe it could have." Jerry threw the envelope back onto the dash and surveyed the car for any missing items. Everything seemed to be in place and cash that he kept for gas still sat in the cup holder between the seats. "That's just weird." He added.

"Do you think someone was in here?"

"Not sure, but I know I left the envelopes on the dash." Jerry looked around the parking lot and noticed an old man washing dishes in a screened in area behind the restaurant.

"Hang here for a second, I'll be right back." Jerry left the car running with Dirk inside and sauntered over in the direction of the screened room. Dirk watched him speak through the screen for a minute or two and saw the old man pointing and saying something. Jerry stared at the shell parking lot as he walked on his way back to the car and sat behind the wheel looking puzzled.

"What's up, what did he say?"

"He said he was threatened by a biker dude with a gun not to say anything!"

Dirk looked at Jerry confused.

"He said it would take more than a revolver to scare him. I think the shotgun leaning against the sink where he was washing pots gave him a little courage as well. He also said the dude sat in the front of my car and went through the papers on the dash. He said he heard him yell something that he couldn't understand and then he threw shells leaving the parking lot.

"Holy crap! That was the guy we saw tear outta here."

"Yep, that was him. He was obviously curious about these papers because he didn't want money." Jerry grabbed the gas money and held it up.

"Okay, now that's weird!" Dirk added.

"Very!" Jerry looked around the car again and slowly pulled out of the parking lot, a little more aware of his surroundings and headed towards Bourg.

@@@@@

Mark brought the Harley to an abrupt stop in the parking lot of Spigots Brew Pub, just up the road from the Jolly Inn and retrieved a cell phone from the inside pocket of his leather coat. He removed his glove and fingered the phone in a purposeful frenzy.

"Hey, I need everything you can find on Penny Myers. Her estate, her worth and see if you can get your hands on the last will and testament. I want to know all of the details." Mark paused and listened.

"I don't give a damn about your excuses!" Mark screamed into the phone then he stroked his long salt and peppered beard as he listened again.

"Did I have excuses when I carried your ass across the desert in Iraq when you were shot? You owe me man!" He raised his voice even more. "Yea, I thought so. I'll be waiting for a call." He slid his phone back into the pocket of his jacket, dismounted the bike and headed to the front door of the brewery. Nobody would recognize him now and he was pretty sure nobody cared anyway.

@@@@@

Dirk caught up on old times with Jerry's older brother, Mike and lied about their plans for the afternoon. With the help of Mike's wife, they packed a small cooler of beer and headed out to the back porch where they sat in the shade and told lies.

"It doesn't look like much has changed around here?" Dirk stated.

"Nope, not really!" Mike agreed. "Minus the chicken coop, a new roof and central heat an air, it's pretty much the same. Just the way we like it. Right bay?" Mike looked over to his wife for assurance.

"Yep, country living at its best." She agreed rolling her eyes.

"So, what brings you to town, Dirk?" Mike was curious.

Dirk and Jerry looked at each other and couldn't hold back the smiles.

"Strangely, the reading of a will." Dirk spoke first.

"Really? I'm sorry, I didn't know one of your relatives passed?" Mike apologized.

"It was Penny Myers!" Jerry interjected.

"Wow! Now there's a name from the past." Mike huffed. "Well, how did it go?"

"Let's just say better than expected." Jerry answered his brother.

"From what I heard, she was loaded? Did she hook you guys up with a little something? I didn't even know you guys knew her that well." Mike fished a little.

"She was very generous!" Jerry answered while Dirk remained quiet.

"How generous?" Mike was more curious now.

"Now Mike, you know I don't like to talk about money, religion and politics. Let's just say she was very generous and keep it at that." Jerry smiled.

Mike looked at them and smiled.

"Okay, we can keep it at that then. Just know that your nieces and nephews would love a pool right back there where the chicken coop was?" Mike said kidding, but not really. After receiving a slap from his wife, Jerry responded.

"Not a problem. I can probably make that happen. You were my favorite brother after all."

"Oh yea, why is that?" Mike laughed.

"You were the only one that didn't beat the crap out of me."

They all laughed and enjoyed a cold beverage for a few minutes until Jerry couldn't wait any longer and spoke up.

"I think I'll take a walk out back to the old barn and reminisce a bit?"

"Why not?" Dirk agreed.

"Try not to get lost or hurt back there you two. You're not as young as you used to be." Mike offered laughing.

Dirk and Jerry followed the fence line as they did so many times before, talking about the differences and changes in the landscape. They both agreed to leave their shoes on this time as their feet weren't as tough as they used to be. They approached the fence and a quiet and calmness overcame them. As they stood at the spot that they had supposedly crossed so many times before, they were speechless. Wire on the fence had deteriorated in spots and broke loose from the posts. Some of the posts had rotted from the ground up and hung there suspended in the air like a levitating magician with skinny arms stretched out to his sides. The barn on the other side of the fence had fallen in disrepair and looked to be abandoned. The once strong and well-kept iron fence that separated the cattle had rusted beyond repair and wild weeds and grass had taken over. Thickets of blackberry vines huddled around the corners of the old barn and hung heavy with clumps of juicy black fruit. They sat in the soft grass and talked about their lives and the things they should have done glancing at the fence now and then.

"It was a stupid idea!" Jerry admitted.

"No, it wasn't man. We are back together catching up and having a few cold beers. It was a great idea." Dirk said reassuring his friend.

"I guess you're right." Jerry agreed.

"However, my butt is going to sleep and it's getting dark. How long you wanna stay?" Dirk asked.

Jerry offered him a hand and they both stood to face the fence one last time. They both lowered their heads, said their own short prayer silently for Penny and turned back towards the house. As they took a few steps away, the two posts held together with three strands of rusted barbed wire, lit up in a sparkling glitter of light behind them. They didn't see it and continued walking until a large crow zipped between their heads, letting out an ear-splitting caw, heading in the direction of the fence. They simultaneously hit the ground and turned to watch the large bird fly right through the wires and disappear beyond the fence.

Prologue

Mark sat behind the wheel of a work truck parked adjacent to Highway 90 and it was slightly hidden from most of the traffic. He had backed in between a large wooden sign and a row of tall weeds, pointing the truck to the East. Mark needed an advantageous view of the cars headed out of town. There was only one road leading to the airport in New Orleans from Houma and he knew they would pass this way. Mark waited for the call, sipped on a coffee and watched every car that passed. An empty box from a 12 pack of beer sat next to him in the front seat, with a few bottles strewn about on the floor board.

It had been a long night of drinking at the small bar off Main Street and his head pounded with pain. The sun was beginning to appear above the tree line and puddles of bright-orange light were scattered across the marsh to the right of him. Mark retrieved his sunglasses from the glove box and placed them over his eyes. The approaching light was not helping with the pain between his ears. He adjusted his glasses slightly and pulled the bill of his hat down to assure no light would get through.

Mark reached for his phone when it began to ring and answered it abruptly.

"Hello?" Mark's voice was cold and raspy. "I'm at the old gas station on Highway 90. Okay I'll be here."

He threw the phone on the seat next to the empty box of beer, sat up in the seat and took another sip of his coffee. Steam poured from the small hole in the lid and the smell of it seemed to sooth him. Within minutes, a white, Chevy Tahoe pulled into the parking lot and a large man approached the driver's door of Mark's truck. He carried a coffee of his own and stood beside the door as Mark lowered the window.

"Where are they?" Mark came right to the point.

"Jerry's vehicle has been parked at ya'll brothers place all night. They got there yesterday afternoon and it hasn't moved since." The man reported.

'They must have really tied one on if they are still there?" Mark said as he ran his fingers through his beard. "Didn't think Mike was much of a drinker anymore?" He added.

"From where I was, I couldn't see too much. It's kind of hard to get close with all the nosey neighbors around there. I did find some information on Mrs. Myers though." The man continued. "Her estate is extremely wealthy and your daughter is the executor. The will was very straight forward except for the part about leaving your brother and his buddy all that money. Not sure of their relationship, but she just made them very rich."

"Yes, I Know. I saw the numbers. It just doesn't make sense."

"What's your next move?" The man asked as he lit a cigarette.

"Well, our next move is to follow those two and find out what the connection is? She gave them the money for a reason and I'm gonna find out why. Dirk should be leaving for Florida soon, now that he has his money.   I'll take a trip over there and dig a little deeper into Dirk's life while you stay here and get everything you can on Jerry. I can't risk being seen by my family around here." Mark explained.

"How long am I going to have to do this?" The man asked agitated.

"Gee, I don't know, how much is your life worth?' It would have been very easy for me to leave you in that bunker in the desert." Mark reminded him again.

"Yea, I get it. You don't have to keep bringing it up. I'll do what I can here." He said, looking over his shoulder then taking a drag from his cigarette. "By the way, why is it so important for you to know what their connection is?

Mark pulled a folded piece of paper from the inside pocket of his jacket and shook it in the air.

"I took this letter from my brother's car. She mentions something about them helping her in some way when she was younger. I want to know what they did that was worth 1.5 million dollars." Mark explained.

The man glanced at the letter and then his attention was directed to the front of the truck. Standing near the front bumper was a little girl who had appeared from nowhere. Her eyes were transfixed on Mark through the windshield and her face was pale white. She slowly raised her hand and placed a small doll on the hood of the truck. Neither of them could speak and the moment caught them both off guard. Walking around the right side of the truck, she passed the passenger door and continued to stare at them. The little girl stopped near the rear bumper, hissed at them like a cat, then vanished into the tall weeds behind the truck.

Made in the
USA
Columbia, SC